Naughty Or Nice

Lauren K. McKellar

16pt

Read How You Want
LARGE PRINT BOOKS, BRAILLE & DAISY

Copyright Page from the Original Book

Title: Naughty or Nice

Copyright © 2019 by LAUREN K. McKELLAR

Published by
Escape
An imprint of Harlequin Enterprises (Australia) Pty Limited (ABN 47 001 180 918), subsidiary of HarperCollins Publishers Australia Pty Limited (ABN 36 009 913 517)
Level 13, 201 Elizabeth St
SYDNEY NSW 2000
AUSTRALIA

romance.com.au/escapepublishing/

TABLE OF CONTENTS

About the author	iii
Acknowledgements	iv
Chapter 1	1
Chapter 2	9
Chapter 3	20
Chapter 4	28
Chapter 5	34
Chapter 6	44
Chapter 7	56
Chapter 8	60
Chapter 9	70
Chapter 10	82
Chapter 11	89
Chapter 12	104
Chapter 13	110
Chapter 14	123
Chapter 15	138
Epilogue	149
Bestselling Titles by Escape Publishing...	154

INTRODUCING

ROMANCE.COM.AU

RURAL | CONTEMPORARY | FANTASY | HISTORICAL | PARANORMAL | ROMANTIC SUSPENSE | LGBTQI

All the books you love with all the romance you need!

Sign up to our newsletter for all the latest romance news, romance e-book deals and competitions!

Naughty or Nice
Lauren K. McKellar

Claire Roberts wants one thing this Christmas: to land the big promotion at work and finally shake free of the office gossip that haunts her. What she doesn't need is more competition, especially from a man who is nothing but trouble.

Hamish Christianson wants one thing this Christmas: to land the big promotion at work so he can support those he loves. What he doesn't need is for his 'nice guy' personality to get in the way, or even worse, to fall for his biggest rival.

With everything on the line, will Hamish and Claire discover what it truly means to win? Or will their naughty games ruin everything?

About the author

LAUREN K. McKELLAR is a writer of contemporary romance reads that make you feel. This hybrid-published best-selling author loves writing books with stunning settings, heart-throb heroes, and leading ladies who overcome great hardships in their lives.

In addition to writing, Lauren loves to read, and you can often find her up at all hours of the night with a glass of wine, some chocolate, and a good book. She lives by the beach in New South Wales, Australia, with her husband, two children, and two dogs. Most of the time, all five of them are well behaved.

If you'd like to know more about Lauren, her books, or to connect with her online, you can follow her on twitter @darragh_lea or like her Facebook page *Lea Darragh Author.*

Acknowledgements

I'd like to thank the lovely team at Escape Publishing, including Kate, for choosing my book for publication. Special thanks also goes to Mimi, for the Christmas decorations, and my beautiful husband, for teaching me that it's always worth believing in yourself, even on the hard days.

For my spirit animals: those people who love Christmas just as much as I do. May your Christmas reads and your Hallmark movies fill your heart with joy.

Chapter 1

Hamish

Nice is my specialty.

Got a kitty needing rescuing from a tree? I do it more often—and looking better—than a fireman.

Have an old lady who needs a hand across the road? Sign me up to your local senior citizens' club, because I am the guy you'll need.

Got a free coffee because the person ahead of you paid it forward? That guy was probably me—and don't worry, you can thank me later.

That niceness doesn't stop in the public eye. I also enjoy being extra nice to the ladies in my life. Call me a traditionalist, but I am a big believer in women going first—through doorways, when speaking, and into orgasm.

That was why I didn't understand Claire Roberts.

I studied the woman at the desk across from me, the jet-black hair that framed the face even blacker than her heart. Ever since I came to work at this firm, she'd made it abundantly clear that she had neither the time nor the inclination to get to know me, despite my many attempts. How could she resist my extreme level of niceness when if you looked the word up in the dictionary, you wouldn't just find a picture of me, but a link to a bible-length appendix citing my virtues?

'Quit staring.' She didn't even look up from her computer screen. How did she do that?

'I'm not staring,' I replied, my eyes still on the evil temptress tap, tap, tapping away at her keyboard. 'I'm admiring your beauty.'

'Can you please admire my beauty from a distance? We have a meeting in'—her eyes flicked from her computer screen down to the phone beside her—'five minutes, and I'm trying to prepare.'

'I could help you with that. I'm very good at preparing. Doing my research.' I paused, staring at her full pink lips. 'I like to give my undivided attention to the project at hand.'

Finally, she met my gaze. Cool green eyes glared at me over the top of the silver rim of her laptop. 'So do I. Which is why I need you to take those bedroom eyes away from my desk.'

'So you think my eyes belong in the bedroom.'

'Yes. *Your own.*' She sighed, but was that a smile lurking at the corner of her lips? 'Can I please just have four-and-a-half more minutes of peace to get this done?'

'Of course.' I pushed back in my chair and took the file from the corner of my desk. As I passed her, I glanced at her screen. A long list of names ran down one side of it. 'Deciding who's been naughty and who's been nice?'

The screen blinked closed in an instant. She swivelled in her chair to glare at me, and this time it wasn't just your average glare—it was next-level, all-out murder. 'Yes. And guess what? You made the cut.'

'Let me guess—you'd like to punish me for my naughty staring ways.' I wiggled my eyebrows, hoping to make her laugh.

'Can you stop being such a sleaze for just one minute?'

'I'm hurt.'

She smiled sweetly, then took her phone and tablet from the desk, standing. The scent of flowers and coffee teased at my nostrils, and damn, that was sweet. 'Yes. You're a sleaze. And just so you know, you made the nice list.'

'Huh. So you're finally seeing what a good guy I can be.'

'It's a different kind of nice list, Hamish.' She stepped past me, her shoulder brushing my arm as she made her way to the printer and slid out a sheet of paper. 'That was a list of people it'd be nice not to have in my life.'

Brutal.

'Tell me, do you break every guy's heart the way you so casually do mine?' I called after her as she walked down the hall.

She didn't reply.

She didn't need to.

Those swinging hips said it all.

It seemed that no matter how hard I tried, how many accounts I landed or how many bonuses I scored, Claire wouldn't give me the time of day, niceness be damned.

'Damn, she's cold.' Zeb gave a low whistle, coming to stand by my side.

'She's ... defrosting,' I said, slowly.

'Well, I'd sure love her to heat things up over in my corner of the office.' He slapped me on the back, then followed Claire down the hall.

I cringed. 'This isn't *Mad Men.*'

'What do you mean?' he asked, stopping in his tracks.

'Maybe you've heard of this little thing called equal rights,' I said, choosing my words carefully. Zeb had been working there a lot longer than I.

'Ha! Yeah, mate, of course.' He started moving again, heading toward the boardroom. 'Come on, mate. I want to get to this meeting on time.'

'*Me too*,' I muttered, the irony of the words clearly lost on him.

A low hum of noise reached my ears as I entered the room. Twelve employees sat around the long oval table, some talking, some looking through their notes. I took a seat between Zeb and Claire at the back, and as Frank walked through the door,

I glanced at my wristwatch. Eleven am. Right on time. Looked like my lunch date would stand after all.

'Got somewhere better to be, Christianson?' Claire asked in a low voice.

I flicked a glance at her. Legs for days stretched under the table beside me. Goddamn. 'Nowhere I'd rather be than here with you.'

'Ha!' She snorted.

'Morning,' Frank muttered, waving hello to the room at large as he shuffled past the black swivel chairs to an empty seat at the head of the table. He pushed his glasses up his nose, the thin frames so at odds with his broad shoulders, his tall physique. 'How are you all today?'

Murmurs of 'good' and 'can't complain' went around the room, and he nodded.

'Right. Excellent.' Frank glanced at a sheet of paper in front of him. 'I have our sales tallies for the month just gone, and you'll all no doubt be unsurprised to know that once again, Hamish has come out on top. Congratulations, Hamish.'

Hell yeah! That made it three months in a row. I beamed. A few polite claps went around the table. Claire stiffened beside me.

'That means you'll get the November bonus. Coming in second was of course Claire—nice work.' Frank nodded in her direction, and she smiled. 'Then Zeb, and the rest of you lot.'

'Congratulations,' I whispered to Claire.

Her eyes didn't move from the man in the front of the room.

'Before we launch into your reports, I want to let you know that there's an opportunity up for grabs at the start of the new year,' Frank said.

I straightened. Opportunity?

'One of you will be promoted to senior accounts manager. Now, in the past we haven't utilised this role, but as we continue to expand I'm beginning to see how it would be an advantage to put one of our top salespeople in a position to motivate and lead others in the team,' Frank continued. 'The person who is awarded this position will be smart, driven, and motivated. Not only will they have excellent and consistent sales figures, but they will be good when it comes to teamwork and skill development.'

I puffed up my chest. It was like he was reading my résumé.

'Of course, there are a few of you I already have in mind for this role, but during the month ahead I will be watching you all closely to see how you perform. I'll announce the promotion Christmas Eve, the day after our Christmas party—which I expect you all to attend, mind you.' He nodded, taking the top piece of paper and moving it to the bottom of the pile. 'Right! Now let's talk budgets.'

Papers shuffled. Voices whispered.

I leaned forward in my seat, my eyes on the man in the front of the room, but my mind on one thought and one thought only.

I had to get that promotion.

Chapter 2

Claire

I had to get that promotion.

Not just because I'd worked here for five years, or because I was good at my job, or because I knew I deserved it.

But because it was getting to the point where I couldn't pay the rent.

'I'm sorry, baby,' Chad had crooned through the phone earlier that morning. 'Just one more month.'

'That's what you said last month. And the month before that,' I'd whispered, glancing over the top of my computer to make sure Hamish wasn't listening. His eyes were focused on his mobile phone. Probably scrolling through social media. 'Chad, this is getting out of control.'

'I know, I know it is. But it's almost a new year! And you know what they say—new year, new you.'

I did. I knew it because that was what he'd said the year before—*new year, new you.* Right before he walked out the door of our shared apartment in the middle of the city, taking the contents of my bank account and my engagement ring with him. 'Chad, please. This is getting out of control. I can't keep covering for you.'

'I don't know what you want me to say. I'm sorry? I'll pay you back?' he'd asked.

'I want you to say "I have the money. It's going into your account next week, and then the bank won't chase you for the overdue amount",' I'd snapped.

'But that would be a lie,' he'd replied, and I'd rested my head in my hands. A lie. Just like our relationship had been. 'I'll have something to you soon, I swear it. On my life, Claire.'

'You better,' I'd replied, trying to inject menace into my tone but no doubt failing miserably.

Now, all I could think about was that promotion. If I landed it, it might be enough to cover the excess debt, at least short-term, or maybe to hire a lawyer and get me out of this mess.

When I took out the loan in my name, I'd thought things between Chad and me were solid. We'd met at work and had been dating for three years, living together for two, and he'd just proposed.

Turned out the money I'd borrowed to finance our wedding and a new car, he'd blown gambling. Right before he blew me off, quitting his job and leaving me with a broken heart and broken bank account courtesy of the debt he'd accrued in my name.

Now I was struggling. A year of making those repayments with little to no help from him, and my purse strings were drawn tight. This was the sort of thing they didn't tell you to look for when you dated. Look for a man who's nice and funny. Someone who pays attention to you and makes you feel special.

No one ever said that a man could be those things, but he could have another side too. One addicted to the rush of gambling, the thrill of risking it all—an affair he'd found all too easy to commit to.

Around me, the room broke into casual chatter as Frank closed the meeting, wishing us all luck for the weeks ahead. December was a busy month, yet one where it was notoriously hard to bring clients in.

'You going to apply for that promotion?' Vi asked as she stood to follow him.

I smiled. 'Definitely.'

'You'll be a shoo-in,' she replied, squeezing my arm. 'I can't think of anyone better suited to the job.'

'Thanks.' I smiled, but I could.

I chanced a quick glance at the man pushing out of his seat to my right. He turned so his butt was eye level, and for a moment, just one moment, I let myself look. I let myself stare at those round globes that I'd heard the women from marketing gossip about on rainy afternoons in the office.

Then I stopped.

Because men who looked like that only broke your heart, and your bank account too.

'You've got time on your side, Claire,' Vi said, pulling my attention back. 'He's only been here three months.'

Three months when he'd consistently come out on top when it came to landing new clients.

'Oh! One more thing!' Frank said, commanding everybody's attention once more. 'We have our office Secret Santa on again. I encourage you all to please get involved. Leave your name with Vi by close of business today if you're interested.'

He turned and left the room, with other members of staff following in dribs and drabs. Vi stood, rushing after her boss. Frank liked a double-shot latte before lunch, but he did not like to be kept waiting.

I stood, collecting my notes and holding them close to my chest. If I wanted a chance at landing that job, I had to work hard, and work fast. There were several new leads I'd been researching, and now was the time to act.

I stopped in the kitchen and placed my notes on the cabinet. Tea. I'd be able to strategise the best game plan with a nice hot cup of tea in my hands.

'Are you going for the promotion?'

I looked up. Hamish leaned against the doorframe, his blue eyes sparking with humour. His tousled dark hair was a devil-may-care twist to his good-boy office attire.

'Yes. Obviously,' I replied, head held high. No point beating around the bush.

'Me too.' He stepped over to the cupboard and pulled a mug out, placing it next to my notes. 'Ah, what's this here? A list of potential—'

'A list of none of your business.' I snatched the folder away. I couldn't afford to let him land any client on there. If they were thinking of coming to our firm, they had to come to me.

'I see you have Actron Energy written down. I actually have a meeting lined up with them myself. Would you like to come?' he asked.

I raised my eyebrows. What was the catch?

'Maybe we could go for a drink after. Get rid of some of this animosity between us,' he continued, and there it was. A date.

Business and pleasure should never mix.

Not even at Christmas.

'I am not going to have a drink with you.' I poured the hot water over my teabag.

'Fine then.' He stood next to me, mixing coffee and sugar in the bottom of his mug. 'Dinner.'

'No!' I turned to stare at him. He was hot—the kind of man women threw themselves at. He had an air of danger about him, wrapped in a shirt and tie.

I glanced down at the knee-length dress that felt a little too tight on me this season, hugging all my curves just that bit too closely. If he was dangerous and sexy, I was girl-next-door and frumpy. We were polar opposites—and men like him didn't go for women like me. All they saw was a meal ticket, someone to play house for them while they went after the next big thing.

Chad's such an arsehole.

I dished sugar into my tea and stirred it angrily.

'I don't know what I have to do to get you to see that I'm a nice guy, but I am.' Hamish held his hands out either side of his body. 'Give me a chance.'

'A chance? A chance to steal my clients out from under me?' A chance to break my heart? 'No way!'

His face darkened. 'If I was worried about stealing clients, I'd just—'

'Hamish. Claire.'

Hamish whirled around. I dropped my spoon.

Frank stood there, his mouth twisted into a scowl of displeasure. 'What's this about stealing clients?'

'It's nothing.' Hamish sighed, turning back to his coffee. 'I was just asking Claire if she wanted to come to a meeting with me this afternoon, and she mentioned that she was concerned it might look like she was stealing my client.'

My grip on my mug tightened. How dare he? Actron was—

It was a client I wanted, yes.

But if Hamish already had a meeting, technically, the client was more his.

'Working together. I like that.' Frank nodded, stepping between us to take his own mug down from the cupboard. 'You know, I think you both are strong candidates for the position we have coming up. But I want to see more from you. More teamwork. More office spirit.' He smiled at me. 'You used to organise all the social goings on around here.'

My chest panged. Used to.

Back when Chad worked at the firm, and I'd been excited about socialising after work.

Back when drinks after meetings with clients weren't a bad thing at all.

'I'll ... I'll make a bigger effort.' I smiled, hoping it was more convincing than I'd thought. 'I'm actually just about to sign up for the Secret Santa.'

'Oh good! Hamish?' Frank asked.

Hamish gave a wide grin. 'Of course. I love Christmas.'

'Don't we all?' Frank chuckled. 'Now, I'll leave you two to prepare for the meeting with Actron. If it does come off, I'm sure we can organise with accounts to split the commission, make it nice and fair.'

He strode out of the kitchen, mug in hand.

I looked up at Hamish. 'Why did you say that?' The client was his, fair and square.

'I thought you might need the extra incentive. To realise I'm a nice guy. That you can trust me,' he said, and there was that word again. *Nice.* Why was he so obsessed with being nice?

'Well, you didn't have to do it. And if you want to take the client for yourself, I'd be okay with that. Obviously.'

'It might be fun to work together for a change.' Hamish shrugged. 'You know—instead of you spending your time trying to break my heart with your constant rejections.'

'Ha!' I rolled my eyes. 'I'm sure there are plenty of ladies to keep that heart intact.'

'No.' He shook his head, that twinkle in his eye again. 'No ladies.'

'No girlfriend?'

'No.'

'No lover?' I pressed.

'No.'

No?

How could a man like Hamish be single?

'If you already have a presentation for Actron, let's use that,' he said, taking his mug and walking out of the kitchen. 'Saves me having to put one together.'

And there it was.

That was how he was single.

He was the kind of guy who made you feel special, wanted, unique—only to get you to invest more into the relationship than he was ever willing to give.

Hamish Christianson was just like my ex.

So why did I find him so attractive?

Chapter 3

Hamish

She was stunning.

There were no two ways about it.

As she stood in front of the two men from Actron, gesturing to the presentation behind her, fire in her eyes and passion in the words that came from her mouth, I knew inviting her to come to this pitch with me was either the best or the worst idea I'd ever had.

The best, because I wanted her. Lust stirred in my veins as she leaned across the table, handing the men and then me a printout, her cleavage hovering right in front of my face.

The worst because she wasn't interested. Not only that, but she was my primary competition when it came to the promotion at work.

That was why I'd invited her here—to show Frank I was all about working as a team. That I wanted the best for the company, not just for my own personal gain.

And I did.

It was just that I wanted my own gain, too. Was that so very wrong?

'And that's why you should choose In The Lead for your marketing in the year to come,' Claire finished up, taking a seat beside me.

'Thank you.' Enrique nodded. 'We appreciate the demonstration. But I have a few questions I was hoping to ask you.'

'Shoot,' she said, smiling.

'Right. As a firm, what would you say your weak points are?' Enrique asked, and I couldn't help but notice that he made eye contact with me as he spoke.

'I'd say our weakest point would be that we care too much.' Claire nailed the question like a pro. 'We want the very best for our clients, so if something isn't working, we put in the extra hours and pull out all the stops to turn it around for them.'

'I see. Hamish?' Enrique pressed.

'Yes?'

'What do you have to say about it?'

My skin prickled. Did it matter what my answer was? 'I agree with Claire. We care a lot about our clients—that's no doubt why we have a ninety per cent retention rate year after year.'

'I see. And what about your strengths? Your ... assets?' He lingered on the word, and for the briefest second his eyes dipped to Claire's chest.

The hairs on the back of my neck rose. Did she see?

'Well, as I said in my presentation, we have a very talented team of people who can meet your needs,' Claire spoke confidently, her eyes never leaving his, but she turned her body slightly toward me, as if protecting herself.

'So that's why I should go with you instead of a bigger firm like Murphy's?' Enrique's eyes lingered on Claire again.

'Actually, Murphy's is downsizing,' I filled in the info on my old place of employment. Looked like I'd left in the nick of time. The EA to the CEO had called to tell me the news on the way to work—how they'd marched a bunch of staff out in the middle of the day, no questions, no pleasantries, and no Christmas bonuses. 'I heard they made some significant staffing cuts this week.'

'I haven't heard anything of the sort.'

'I doubt they'd include it in their pitch. Which company would it make you more likely to sign with? One worried about internal budgets? Or one focused on ensuring your marketing budget received the biggest bang for each buck spent?' I asked.

Enrique's black eyes glittered. 'I see. And if this was to go ahead, who would be my point of contact? You?' Enrique looked at Claire, and something in his gaze ... 'Or you?' He turned to me.

'We...?' Claire paused.

'We both would,' I offered.

'Sounds confusing,' Enrique replied.

'Sounds like between the two of us, there'd always be someone available to help you with your needs.' I leaned forward across the table. I'd met guys like him before—ones who'd already made a decision but wanted you to jump through hoops. 'Listen, I know you're a busy man, and we have other clients to see too. How about any further questions you pop in an email, and we can discuss it further?'

'So you're too busy for me.' Enrique leaned back in his seat.

'Never too busy,' Claire rushed. Damn it! Didn't she know that made us look desperate?

'Then why do you have to leave?' Enrique asked.

'As I said, I have another meeting this afternoon. But let's chat in the weeks ahead,' I said. *If you haven't found another marketing agency who'll let you squeeze them like a snake first.* Clients like him were hard work, and rarely worth the pain.

'Can we be flexible on price, Claire?' Enrique asked, as if I hadn't spoken a word.

'We could certainly look at tailoring the plan to suit your budget,' she said, gathering her things. 'We'll talk about it over email, or—'

'Claire,' I growled. We were a team.

'I would be happy to talk to you on the phone,' she finished, flicking me a look that was definitely not so nice.

'Thank you for your time today, gentlemen.' I extended my hand for the two men to shake, and Claire followed suit.

Frosty silence walked with us all the way to the lift, then the whole ride down to the taxi rank.

When we were seated inside a cab headed back to In The Lead, she finally spoke.

'You blew it in there. Too busy to answer a few questions?' she asked, her full lips tightened to a thin line.

'It was strategy, Claire. Men like that like to be kept waiting. They think they're all-important, and if you give too much at first, they dig for more.'

'If that was the strategy, why didn't you tell me before we went in?'

'I didn't know that was what they'd be like till we met,' I replied. 'What do you think I am? A mind-reader?'

'Clearly not,' she snorted. 'But you cut me off when I was speaking! You made me look like a child.'

I opened my mouth to protest, then snapped it shut. I hadn't meant to—had I done that? I'd been so caught up in the moment, and then when Enrique had stared at her chest ... Anger boiled my blood. I couldn't exactly tell her that.

I turned to stare out the window. 'For one minute, can you just give me a break?'

Traffic merged into a single lane as we wound around tall buildings that stretched up toward the sky like long grey fingers. Overhead, grey clouds were moving in. 'Silent Night' played on the radio, a small hint of warmth in an otherwise frosty environment.

'You made me feel like an idiot.' Her voice was small. 'And I don't like being spoken to like that.'

I glanced over. Gone was the stormy veneer from moments earlier. Her eyes were soft, vulnerable. Her chest rose and fell slow, deep, as if each breath cost her a lot. My fingers itched to touch her, run my thumb over that rosebud mouth and kiss the smile back on her face. Where was the woman from half an hour earlier, the one who owned that boardroom with her fiery passion? She'd been prepared to give her all to win that client. She'd been *alive.*

'You were amazing in there, Claire,' I said, keeping my hands in my lap. 'Your presentation was great. If they don't sign based on that alone, they're idiots.'

A small smile lifted her lips. 'Thank you.'

We rode in silence the rest of the way back to the office.

Chapter 4

Claire

I loved Christmas.

I loved the way it smelt—like pine trees, and spun sugar, and women's perfume in the air.

I loved the way it tasted—like nutmeg, and ginger, and sparkling wine, a combination of richness and celebration all at once.

I loved the way it sounded—like bells, and laughter, and the Health Direct Christmas Carols that played on television every year.

I loved the way it looked—like fairy lights, and bright red gift-wrap, and mistletoe.

But mostly, I loved the way it felt.

Like *home.*

Like a home I missed so very much.

'Have you finished all your shopping for the year?' Vi asked, stopping to hold open the door at the grand old department store in the mall.

I followed her inside, the building's air-conditioning a pleasant relief from the sultry summer heat. 'Mostly. I just need to pick up something else for Mum...'

'Perfume?' Vi gestured to the pinks, purples, golds, and greens of the bottles dotted over the glass counters in front of us. 'Everyone loves perfume.'

'Maybe...' I picked up the nearest one—Wild Rose. My finger pumped down the nozzle and the scent of old-lady potpourri filled the air. I coughed, choking on the pungent aroma, and put the bottle down. 'Definitely not.'

'How are you feeling, anyway? I know this is only your second Christmas without Chad—'

'I'm fine.' I shrugged the question off.

'Are you sure? You were together three years. And holidays like this—they can make you wish you had someone.'

'Well, not me. I'm fine.' I pressed the button for the lift.

'You never want to talk about him, but I know he's still a big part of your life.' Vi's eyes were kind as her hand touched my arm. 'Don't you want to vent? To let someone in?'

I shrugged. I'd let Chad in. That had been problem enough. 'Vi, you are too good to me. But honestly, I'm doing okay. It's just Christmas.'

The lie tasted sour in my mouth.

As the lift shot up to the building's fourth floor, Vi took out her phone. I kept my eyes on the little numbers above the door.

'Oh! Secret Santa emails are in!' She nudged my shoulder as the doors opened, taking us out to the womenswear department.

'Already?' I'd forgotten about that. Just one more hoop to jump through to try and get this promotion.

'Yeah.' She made a face. 'Ugh. I have Frank. What am I supposed to get him?'

'A Christmassy tie?' I offered.

'Oh God! Yes, I should. Something ridiculous. Who'd you get?'

I slipped my hand into my bag and pulled my phone out. We strolled past a rack of long, slinky black dresses, and Vi paused, pulling one out to admire.

'What do you think? I can see you in this at the Christmas party,' she said.

I looked up. Red beading decorated the neckline, making the dress look as if it were alight. The dress scooped low in the back, then dropped to the floor in a combination that was somehow sinful, sweet, and sexy all at once. *I love it.*

I glimpsed the price tag.

I hated it.

I hated it more than I hated Chad, and debt collectors, and men who tried to stop me from getting what I wanted.

'I don't know. I think I'll just wear something I already have,' I hedged, focusing back on my phone, eager for the distraction.

'What? But this would look amazing on you,' Vi said.

My heart stopped.

My Secret Santa email had arrived.

'I got Hamish.' I held my phone out miserably. 'But I presume you already knew that.'

'It's a random generator. I may have taken the names, but I had no idea who ended up with who.' Vi held up one hand. 'Scout's honour.'

'Ugh,' I groaned. 'What on earth am I going to get him?'

I pressed my eyes closed, stared up at the ceiling. Could this week get any worse?

Today, four days after the meeting with Actron, the client had called—called Hamish, not me—and asked if he could come meet with them a second time. *Alone.*

Of course, I'd told him to go. After all, it wasn't like I could force them to work with me.

But the snub still burned, reminded me that he was my main competition for this promotion, and at the rate he was going, he'd blitz me when it came to the finish line.

What I needed was a big win. Someone bigger than Actron. Someone like—

'Health Direct!' I exclaimed, shoving my phone back in my bag.

Vi looked at me as if I'd lost my marbles. 'Uh ... you okay?'

'They would be the perfect client. Health Direct,' I repeated.

'The Christmas Carols sponsor?' Vi asked, and I nodded. 'But they've been with Murphy's for years, haven't they?'

'Yes.' I grinned. 'But Murphy's is downsizing. Maybe they'd be open to a move.'

'They would be amazing,' Vi's eyes widened. 'You know, I have a cousin who works there. I could try get you a meeting.'

'That would be amazing,' I gushed. 'Thank you.'

'No worries.' Her eyes sparked with amusement. 'As for Hamish ... you could always get him a lump of coal. He's the sort of man I wouldn't mind putting on my naughty list.'

I rolled my eyes. 'Well, you can keep him there,' I said, running one hand along a silk scarf my mother would love. 'He's not the sort of man I'd date—now or ever.'

'Okay.' Vi shrugged, but even though she didn't speak, I felt the full force of her argument.

Chapter 5

Hamish

Half past twelve.

Time for my standing lunch date.

Only she was running late, and at this time of year, with this much on the line, I didn't have time to lose.

I glanced out the window, past the Christmas lights twinkling there, and to the street. A mass of people walked past, but I couldn't see her. No wild red hair. No loud voice calling across the room.

'Sorry, sorry, sorry.'

I looked left.

Renee rushed toward me from the elevator. She navigated around a few people stopped beside the menu outside the cafe and pressed a kiss to my cheek. 'I couldn't get a park, and then by the time I dropped Harry off—'

'It's fine.' I waved her apology away. 'I ordered you the Caesar salad.'

'Hold the anchovies?' She narrowed her eyes.

'Do you think I'm some kind of sadist?' I asked. 'Of course I held the anchovies.'

'Thank goodness.' She swiped at her forehead, as if the narrowly escaped Death by Sardine was truly a moment for concern. 'You know if they'd been left in, I'd have to order again.'

'That or call the poison squad.' I nodded sagely, holding out her chair for her before sitting at the place opposite.

'Obviously,' she replied.

'How is Harry today?' I asked.

'Good. He's just having a quick check-up with the doctors upstairs; nothing serious, all routine. Oh! And he loves the new car you bought him last week.'

I smiled, thinking of the cute kid's face lighting up when I'd presented it to him as an early Christmas present. I'd give him the world if I could.

It was just a shame the one thing I most wanted to give him was out of my reach.

'So tell me, how's the quest for the promotion? Going well?' Renee asked, changing the subject.

'I think so.' It was only one week after Frank had made his big announcement, but already I'd signed on a new client, and renewed another. The problem was they'd both been small fish. What I needed was an Actron, a monolith, someone with big marketing dollars to spend, to really get me across the line.

That and a reprieve from my guilt.

Ever since Enrique had asked to see me, and me alone, I couldn't shake the feeling of wrong from my shoulders—as if I were betraying Claire by going solo.

'Uh-uh. I know that look.' Renee circled her finger around my face. 'There's a girl.'

'The only woman in my life is you. You know that.'

'Hamish...' Renee placed her hand over mine, resting it on the table. 'There's a girl.'

I grinned. 'There might be a girl—'

'I knew it!'

'—but she's my colleague, and my primary competition for the promotion at work,' I said. 'And to top it all off, she's immune to my charms. My nice ways. There's no chance of anything happening there.'

'Oh Hamish. Ye of little faith.' Renee shook her head dramatically, just as the waiter hovered over our table, two plates in hand.

'One Caesar salad, and one turkey toastie.' He placed them down in front of us, then left.

'You got turkey?' Renee wrinkled her nose.

'It's Christmas.' I shrugged. 'Turkey is festive.'

'I forgot how much you Christianson boys love Christmas.' She smiled, and a wistful expression crossed her face. 'There's so much I forget sometimes.'

'Hey.' I reached over the table and squeezed her shoulder. 'You're allowed to forget things like that. That's not important.'

'It is.' She shrugged me off. 'That's the kind of thing that *makes* a person.'

'No.' I shook my head. 'What makes a person are the bigger things. Like being kind. Caring. Nice.'

'You're too broad scale.' She smiled, but her eyes retained that sad sheen. 'They're not specific—those terms could apply to anyone. What makes a person is loving Christmas. It's running into the waves at full speed because you don't want to chicken out in front of your family.'

I smiled. *Josh, running into the waves, Renee standing on the beach and squealing as the cool water lapped at her toes.* 'He always did love to do that, didn't he?'

She smiled. 'He did. He used to say it was the ultimate battle of mind over matter.'

Mind over matter.

That was my brother's motto, right until the end.

'Anyway, all this is beside the point. Tell me about the girl.' Renee waved the conversation away.

'Like I said—there isn't really a girl.' I picked up a piece of my sandwich. 'At least, not in the romantic sense, anyway.'

'I don't know.' Renee stabbed at a piece of lettuce with her fork. 'You said she's competition for the promotion. That must mean she's ambitious, talented—aren't they qualities you'd look for in a partner?'

'Well, yes.' I frowned. 'But in an ideal world, my ambitious and talented hypothetical girlfriend doesn't want my job.'

'But this world isn't ideal, Hamish.' Renee sighed, and for a moment, I saw the pain of losing her husband painted on her face. So strong. She was the strongest woman I knew.

Thirteen months ago, my brother and their four-year-old son, Harry, had been in a car crash. The other driver had been on ice. He was sent to jail for five years and suffered a broken leg.

Harry had had lacerations to his liver, and internal bleeding that still required constant check-ups even to this day.

My brother had died.

The world was far from ideal. We knew that better than anyone.

Renee pasted on a smile, moving the conversation along. 'As for her being a colleague, that just makes things more interesting. Does your work have a policy on dating?'

'I don't think so.' I couldn't remember reading anything about it in the employee handbook. 'But are policies like that ever set in stone? I thought it was just understood: thou shalt not date thine colleague.'

'And "thou shalt not eat the yoghurt in the fridge if thine does not own it".' Renee's eyes sparked.

'And "thou shalt label all thine food in case thine tuna sandwich looks too similar to Jerry's".' I laughed along with her.

'But see, these commandments—they're not losing-your-job-over offences. That's why they're not in the handbook,' Renee said.

'That doesn't mean you should do them.'

'And it doesn't mean you should not.'

I took a bite of my sandwich, mulling over her words. Did she have a point? Maybe, but there was still one vital problem—Claire didn't like me. It was as simple as that; she'd made it abundantly clear. And while we seemed to have formed some kind of truce since that moment in the car on the way back from Actron, I still wasn't sure where I stood.

I blinked. Was that—?

Claire.

There she was.

She stood at the entrance to the cafe and clutched a manila folder to her chest, those touchable curves that I ached to caress. Her green eyes roamed over the tables before stopping on one near the back. She waved at a woman with dark curly hair and shrewd beady eyes, and I watched her walk over, shake her hand, and sit down.

'Hello? Earth to Hamish?' Renee waved a hand in front of my face. I hadn't even realised she was talking.

'Sorry.' I took one last glance at Claire. She opened her folder, tucked a lock of hair behind her ear. Hair that I could imagine splayed out over my sheets. Hair I wanted to tangle my hands in again and again.

'You're looking at that woman like she's the tastiest thing you've ever seen.'

'That's her. That's Claire.'

'The one talking to the hospital's marketing manager?' Renee asked.

I jerked my head back to her. 'What?'

'That's Marie Foster. Health Direct's marketing manager,' she replied, matter-of-factly. 'I know, because she came to ask us to sign a waiver the other day for Harry to appear on television. They're filming the weather segment here or something.'

Claire was meeting with Health Direct Hospital.

She was trying to land their marketing.

That was ballsy. Health Direct had been with Murphy's for years. To get them on board would be a big coup, and one that Frank couldn't miss.

But it was also dangerous. When I'd worked with Murphy's, their contracts had been watertight. Even if they had downsized, there wouldn't be a way for Claire to bring this hospital over without someone at Murphy's making a very big mistake—and Murphy's staff rarely made mistakes.

I needed to let Claire know. She needed that information in order to form a strong plan of attack

'I'll be back.' I stood, my chair scraping over the tiled floor of the cafeteria.

'You go break those office commandments, Hamish!' Renee called as I walked away from the table, but I didn't smile.

I wouldn't let anyone hurt Claire Roberts.

Not if I could help it.

Chapter 6

Claire

'Is this seat taken?'

I froze. Every hair on my skin, every nerve ending in my body, stood on end.

What fresh hell was this?

I looked up. Hamish towered over the table, that charming smile in place, his blue eyes twinkling brighter than the Christmas lights draped around the windows of the room.

'Hamish,' I said, pasting on a wide grin. 'Fancy seeing you here.'

Subtext: there's nothing fancy about it, and how the hell did you know where I'd be?

'It's strange who you meet in hospital cafeterias, isn't it?' He cocked his head to the side, then held out his hand to the woman sitting across the table from me. 'Hi, I'm Hamish. Hamish Christianson.'

'Marie Foster,' the woman simpered, and it was all I could do not to roll my eyes. *Yes, he's good looking, but that doesn't mean you have to turn into a puddle of goo when he makes eyes at you.*

'I work with Claire,' Hamish continued, entirely focused on Marie. 'We spend a lot of time together.'

'I can imagine that would be quite pleasurable,' Marie said, and why was she still holding his hand?

'It certainly is.' Hamish finally—*finally*—drew his fingers from her grasp and gestured to the empty chair again. 'Would you mind if I joined you?'

'Of course not.' Maree pulled the corner of the seat from the table, allowing Hamish to just slide right in. *Jerk.* 'Any partner of Claire's is more than welcome.'

'He's not my partner,' I blurted out. Both heads snapped at me, as if I'd dragged them from their flirty reverie by the ends of their hair. 'We just work together. In the same office. Near each other.'

'My desk is right *over* from hers,' Hamish said, and I could practically see the wheels in Marie's head turning. *Over her.* What would Hamish look like, naked and hovering over her?

'Marie and I were just talking about a possible move to In The Lead,' I said, filling Hamish in. 'I was outlining some of the many benefits of working with our group.'

'She mentioned you have great personal service and attention to detail.' Marie directed that line at Hamish.

I was going to be sick. I was going to vomit the sandwich I'd wolfed down in the cab on the way over here all over the two of them.

'I assure you, we cover everything so our clients are completely satisfied,' Hamish played right into her hands. 'But tell me, isn't Health Direct already in bed with someone else?'

Warning bells sounded. Marie's eyes flashed with something—concern?—then she straightened, a frosty expression taking over her face.

'We can talk about that later,' I said, because that had been my plan. Win her over with our services, then bring her back to reality—you can't have any of this unless you let go of Murphy's and sign with us.

'I don't know. I think we should put all our cards on the table now.' Hamish rapped against the white tabletop with his knuckles. 'You're with another marketing company. We're better. I used to work at Murphy's, and I can say that unequivocally.'

'You're cocky,' Marie said, her eyes now clear of that lust haze.

'No. Just honest.' Hamish shrugged. 'But because I used to work there, it means I also know what sort of contract they'd have you tied up in. I don't know that you'd be in a position to just up and change firms at the drop of a hat.'

Marie seemed to consider his words, nodding slowly.

'But the firm she signed with isn't the firm she's getting,' I blurted. Why was he doing this? Surely Health Direct had a legal team who could sort out those sorts of details.

'It is, Claire. The number of staff may be different, but trust me, those contracts are watertight,' he said.

Maree's back stiffened. She directed her icy gaze on me. 'When you set this meeting up, you said you knew my situation.'

'I did, I—'

'So what you're saying is you organised this meeting to waste my time.'

'What? No!' My jaw dropped.

'It was lovely to meet you, Claire. Hamish.' Marie nodded to each of us as her chair screamed along the tiled floor.

I rushed to my feet, stepping into her path. 'Please, Marie, let's talk some more.'

'Let me look at the contract,' Hamish said, seemingly unfazed.

Marie's glare was withering. 'Why would I do that?'

'Because I know Murphy's. I'll help you get out of the contract without any legal ramifications,' he said, cool as you like.

'I'm sure Marie's legal team are more than capable of handling a little thing like contracts,' I said.

Marie sighed, shaking her head. 'They are, but we're a hospital. Our legal team is run off their feet, especially at this time of year.' She paused. 'I have to say, I did like a lot of your ideas, Claire. And I think your team is certainly appealing.'

Hamish dipped his head graciously at the compliment.

'Why don't I have a copy of the contract emailed over for you to have a look at? If you can find a way around it, we can take discussions from there.' Maree slipped her hand into her black pantsuit, pulling out a small white card. 'Here's my email and phone. Get in touch when you have a concrete package with a concrete solution.'

'Thank you.' Hamish got to his feet, pocketing the card and extending his hand once more. 'It was lovely to meet you.'

'Lovely to meet you too.' She smiled, then turned to me, shaking my hand before marching around groups of people toward the lift.

I turned my glare on Hamish, my arms folded across my chest. 'What the hell was that?'

'I was looking out for you before you made a promise you couldn't keep,' he hissed, a cold light in his eyes.

'I didn't promise anything.' I gathered up my folder, tucking it under my arm, and strode toward the lift.

'You didn't, but you could have put her in a really difficult position. She works for a hospital, Claire. What if she signed with us and put her company in breach?'

I made a face, jabbed the button for the elevator to go down. 'She's a grown-up. She has lawyers. She would have figured it out.'

'But at what cost?' Hamish shook his head. 'There are hundreds of different companies in the city. I don't know why you had to go after this one.'

The elevator dinged open and I strode inside, pressing the button for the parking lot below. 'And I don't know why, with hundreds of companies in the city, you had to go after the one client I wanted to get.'

'I didn't! I was just trying to help!' Hamish raised his voice as the doors closed, leaving us trapped in the small space.

'By following me! By stalking me through the city and trying to steal what's mine!' I protested, whirling on him.

'You think I followed you?' His eyes glittered. 'I'm not crazy!'

'No, you're not. You're a guy who thinks he can use his good looks to get away with whatever the hell he wants.' I stepped closer, poking a finger at his chest. 'I've met guys like you before, and let me tell you, you won't come out ahead. These underhanded tactics—'

'Underhanded?'

'—never work,' I snapped.

My gaze dropped to my hand, still against his chest. His hard, solid chest. I looked up, and his eyes were softer now, without the fire that had flamed there before. My mouth felt dry, and the words that had been just there on the tip of my tongue fell away to nothing.

'Don't tell me what to do.' His voice was low, predatory. His hand grabbed the back of my head, threaded through my hair.

'Then don't—'

His lips crashed into mine.

I froze. What was he—

His mouth, so hot, so warm, kissed me. He grasped me to him, pulled me closer as if I were his oxygen and he were desperate for air.

Want unfurled inside me, a hungry beast ready to be unleashed. My folder dropped to the floor. I ran my hands over his back, those broad shoulders—divine. His tongue traced across the seam of my lips, and they parted, granting him entrance. The hand at the small of my back jerked my body forward until I felt his need hard up against me, and I shivered. More. This. *Yes.*

'Claire,' he groaned as he kissed along my jaw, tangling his hand in my hair. A ferocious cocktail of pleasure and pain shot through me, and I moaned my want, my need, my—

'Mummy, what are dat man and wady doing?' a small voice asked.

Oh, no.

I pushed at Hamish's chest, then jumped to the other side of the elevator. We'd arrived at our destination—only neither of us had seemed to realise.

A woman and a little girl stood in the parking lot, open-mouthed.

'They were just getting out of the lift,' the woman snapped, her gaze pure murder.

'Sorry,' I murmured, running a hand over my clothes. I scrambled to pick up the scattered paper, my folder, and walked out of the lift, my head held as high as I could.

'Sorry.' Hamish's voice sounded behind me, but I didn't look as I marched toward my car. My cheeks flamed. How embarrassing.

What had I been thinking? I wasn't even attracted to the man and his smarmy ways, his cocky attitude, and his—

That tongue, lashing against my own. The way he'd felt against me, all hard, all man.

'Claire, wait.' He gripped my arm, and I turned around.

His eyes were still dark with desire, and I wanted to give in—wanted to grab him by the tie and drag him into my car. Wanted him to take me because need, raw and feral, raged through my body like I couldn't remember it doing before. For so long, I'd been focused on work, and I'd turned off these feelings—now it seemed they'd all come unstuck.

'I'll meet you back at the office,' Hamish said.

My stomach turned to lead.

Of course.

The office.

It was just a kiss. It wasn't the start of something more, and it even if it had been, was that what I really wanted?

No.

Yes.

My heart went into freefall. 'Fine,' I said, holding my head high. 'Make sure you send me that contract when Maree emails it across to you, too.'

His eyes searched my face. I could see the 'sorry' in his expression. *He's going to apologise.*

No.

He couldn't do that.

That would make that one kiss, that one mistake, seem even worse than it already did.

'Claire, I—'

I held up my hand, shaking my head. 'Just don't.'

He scrubbed a hand over his stubbled jaw, looking into my eyes for the longest time.

Then he turned on his heel and walked away.

I headed toward my car, keeping my head high, but I hated the sting that pricked at the backs of my eyes. I hated Hamish. I had ever since he came to work at In The Lead. One kiss had been a mistake—a moment of weakness after three months loaded with tension, with push and pull, with give and take.

One kiss didn't mean anything.

But as I unlocked my car, I couldn't quiet the other voice in my head.

One kiss meant the world.

Chapter 7

Claire

Every time I closed my eyes, it was there.

That kiss.

That kiss I wanted so badly to forget and relive all at once.

I glanced around the living room. An empty bucket of Ben & Jerry's rested on the coffee table. My bra was draped over the arm of the living room chair, and an open packet of Doritos beckoned me from the table, the lights from my Christmas tree turning the foil green then red as they flashed. In the background, the television played reruns of *The Bachelor.*

My stomach churned, not just from emotional queasiness but from actual overindulgence, and I groaned. Ugh. Why did I do this to myself?

My phone rang from its spot on the coffee table, and I groaned again. Of all the times...

'Chad. Hi,' I said, trying to inject a sense of normalcy into my tone.

'Are you okay?' His voice was full of concern.

'I'm fine.'

'Are you sure?' he asked.

'Positive.'

'How many tubs of ice cream before you took off your bra?' he asked, and damn it. That was the downside to dating someone for three years—they knew you well, even when you didn't want them to.

'Just one. But it was diet.' *Lies.*

'I'm sure it was.' Chad chuckled knowingly. 'It's nearly Christmas, babe. You love this time of year too much to be spending your days surrounded by junk food and bad reality TV.'

'It's...' I shook my head, clearing the junk-food-induced haze. This was my ex—a man who'd betrayed me. He didn't get to lecture me on what I should and shouldn't be doing in any aspect of my life. 'Chad, if you'd just pay me some of what you owed me, maybe I'd never have had to end up in a position like this.'

'I'm sorry, Claire. Really, I am. It's why I'm calling.' He paused, as if leading to some big news. 'I have a new job.'

'Really? That's great,' I said. 'So you can start repayments soon?'

'Yes. Next month I'll be golden, I swear it.' The excitement in his voice was contagious. 'I'll pay double from then until the end of the loan, then I'll keep up the repayments until you're square. Not only that, but I'll send you some money next week, just before Christmas. Like a bonus, to say thanks again for helping me out this past year.'

'That would be...' *Great. Amazing. A dream come true.* 'Just see how you go, Chad,' I finished with instead.

'I won't let you down, Claire. Not this time. This time, things are different,' he said, energy in his voice. In the background, a car honked. 'Shoot, I gotta go. Just wanted to call and tell you the good news.'

'Thank you.'

'And whatever happened, just remember that you can handle it, okay?' he asked, and I forced a smile.

'Okay,' I said.

We ended the call, and I placed the phone back on the table, my heart somehow heavier than it was before.

This wasn't the first time I'd received a call like that.

It was the first time I didn't believe his promises though. He'd let me down too many times before.

Still, he was right about one thing.

I could handle it.

I'd been handling things before, and I could do it again. I just needed to focus on work. To land Health Direct. To get this promotion.

And to forget all about my sexy co-worker.

That item was top of my list.

Chapter 8

Hamish

Hamish: *Hey Claire. Sorry to bother you on the weekend, but I just wanted to let you know that Health Direct sent the contract through. I'll look it over tonight.*

Claire: *Thanks for letting me know. Give me a call if there's anything you need.*

I stared at the blinking cursor on my screen. Anything I needed.

I could think of one thing I needed right now, but it had little to do with contracts and paperwork, and everything to do with the sexy co-worker I hadn't been able to get off my mind all week.

Her hot body. Those delicious curves pressed up against me...

I closed my eyes, savoured the memory for what had to be the hundredth time since it happened. That kiss had been explosive. Everything I could have wanted.

But ever since it happened, Claire had been even more closed off than usual.

Back at work, I'd tried to bring up the subject of the kiss more than once and each time, she'd shut me down, quickly. She'd made it abundantly clear—that kiss was something she didn't want to speak, think, or hear about, ever again.

Or maybe it was me. Maybe I'd done something to piss her off. Maybe she'd wanted to take things further once we got into the parking lot, finish what we'd started in the back of her car.

I stifled a laugh. There was wishful thinking if ever I'd heard it. A woman like her was too good for a one-and-done in a car. A woman like her would be used to champagne and roses, lovemaking on thousand-thread-count sheets.

I glanced across at my own bed. When was the last time I washed those?

I lifted up one corner of the linen, took a sniff.

Too long.

Way too long.

Still, as I balled the material up and stuffed it in the machine, Claire lingered in my mind.

I sank onto the sofa, pulling my phone from my pocket once more, and typed out another message.

Hamish: *The only thing I need is...*

I stopped before I hit send. What I needed was her body, pressed against mine. My hands under that tight shirt. Her coming undone around me as I kissed along the creamy skin of her neck.

Hamish: *The only thing I need is your gratitude when I help land you the biggest client our firm has ever seen.*

Better. Not entirely true, but better.

Claire: *You may have helped, but you also hindered. It was you who brought this whole contract thing up in the first place.*

Hamish: *I just didn't want to see you in trouble. I was trying to be nice.*

Claire: *What is it with you and nice? Always so nice.*

I sighed, walked to the fridge, and grabbed a beer. What was I supposed to say to that?

I spent the next three hours studying the Murphy's contract. As I'd suspected, it was tight—watertight—and I didn't see how Health Direct could get out of it. Claire was going to be disappointed. She couldn't sign them—not now. Not until the Murphy's contract finished in six months' time.

By then it will be too late.

Too late for the promotion, and likely too late for Claire.

I forced a smile. That should have been good news for me. I needed that job more than she did. It had to be mine.

I grabbed some clean sheets from the hamper, laid them out on the bed. With Actron under my belt, Claire would find it hard to top my sales for the month. The only way she could beat me was if Health Direct came on board, and as per usual, it looked like Murphy's had locked their client down behind an impenetrable wall. Health Direct wouldn't be able to get out of it unless Murphy's made some kind of mistake.

But what if they already have?

I flicked the top sheet over the mattress. It didn't matter. It didn't matter if they already had, because I wasn't going to pursue that—not for Claire. Not when it put something I wanted, something I needed, in so much jeopardy.

What if a mistake has been made—a breach of contract—and the client just hadn't realised?

I grabbed my phone, tapped out a message. Darcy and I had once been pretty close—and better yet, the beautiful executive assistant for Mr Murphy himself owed me a favour.

Hamish: *Hey, Darc. I'm doing some investigating into Health Direct. Remember that favour you owe me?*

Seconds later, the reply came in.

Darcy: *You ask someone to feed your cats while you go on holidays once, and they laud it over you for the rest of your life.*

Hamish: *A pretty pussy deserves a pretty favour.*

Darcy: *Uh-uh. No. Your flirting is no good here.*

Hamish: *That wasn't flirting. If I was flirting with you, you'd know it.*

Darcy: *If you were flirting with me, I wouldn't just look into Health Direct for you, I'd book you an appointment, because you'd obviously need your head read.*

Darcy: *I'll log onto the online system and look into Health Direct for you. But please, never sleaze near me again. You make me feel so dirty.*

Hamish: *Thanks, Darcy. You're the best. And don't worry about the dirty thing—I'm sure Veronica will help wash you clean again.*

I sank back into the couch. Hopefully, she'd be able to dig up something good.

I wanted to help Claire—wanted her to land this account.

But I need that promotion.

Not someone else.

Not Claire.

I tried to push down that voice in the back of my head, but it was there.

So were the bills on the end of the coffee table. I lifted one up, my eyes fixed on the five figures down the bottom of the page. A red *overdue* stamp was printed over the top. Damn it. This one couldn't wait much longer.

Flickers of red teased me from farther down the pile. Neither could any of them. It might have been Christmas, but debt collectors didn't believe in the season for giving. There was no give—it was all take, take, take.

I sipped at the beer, but it tasted too bitter, too sour in my mouth. What was I doing? Why was I giving a perfectly good lead to a woman, just because she'd somehow become stuck in my head?

'Damn it,' I whispered, pinching at the bridge of my nose.

Bed. I'd go to bed and deal with this—sort out some kind of game plan for what would happen if I didn't get this job—in the morning.

As I placed the most pressing bill back on the pile, the letters shifted. Behind them, the silver corners of the photo frame caught the overhead light.

Don't do it. You don't need to do this.

With one shaking hand, I pulled the photo closer.

Two smiling faces looked up at me from the frame, identical grins that stretched wide across sun-loved faces. Slowly, I traced one finger over my brother's nose, his blue eyes, the freckles that dotted his cheeks—the only difference between us.

My chest constricted, that familiar ball of pain always lurking under the surface. I pressed my eyes closed tight for a moment. Christmas.

Lights draped around trees.

Presents in brightly coloured paper.

Carols in the park, in buildings, on the television.

Family.

It was always so much harder at Christmas.

I dropped the photo on the couch. Fuck that. Fuck Christmas, and fuck the world.

As I made my way to the bedroom, my phone beeped.

Darcy: *Found something interesting. Am sending you an email now. Consider all pussy-related favours coming to a close.*

A small smile flickered on my lips.

Hamish: *Thanks, Darcy. You're the best.*

This was what I needed. And maybe I could talk to Claire about going halves in the commission. If Darcy was as good as her word, this client would only be signing with us because of something I'd brought to the table. Fair was fair, after all.

But as I brushed my teeth, splashed water over my face, and stared at those tired, unsmiling eyes in the mirror, I couldn't stop the doubt racing through my mind.

Would I really ask that?

Would I really do it?

I walked into the bedroom, slipped off my clothes, and tossed them in the hamper. I had to. I had to do it, or everything would fall apart. I needed the money, goddamn it. This was no time for playing nice. You didn't leave Murphy's to come to In The Lead and fail.

Health Direct was mine. There were no two ways about it.

Yet as my head hit the pillow, my fingers typed the message anyway.

Hamish: *Got some news about Health Direct. Want to meet tomorrow morning for coffee to discuss?*

Claire: *That's fantastic! Maybe you really are a nice guy after all.*

I stared at those words. You really are a nice guy.

If only she knew just how how nice.

Chapter 9

Claire

What did you wear to a coffee meeting on a Sunday with a man you hated but had accidentally kissed in a moment of weakness, who you now owed a favour to?

I glanced down at the sky-blue wrap dress, the frill on the skirt dancing in the summer breeze.

Apparently, you dressed as if you were going on a date.

Why did I choose this? I should have worn a shirt, letting him know I meant business. And a jacket. And maybe a chastity belt.

But what if it is a date?

I pursed my lips. I hated that thought.

But it was there. And I couldn't stop thinking about just what coffee on a Sunday was really supposed to mean.

I glanced at the busy cafe, searching for a familiar face in the crowd. White tables were strewn across the sidewalk, crowded with people sipping their lattes and soaking up the gorgeous morning sun. Waiters bustled from group to group balancing plates and menus and mugs. *It's probably busy because everyone wants to get their caffeine fix before Christmas shopping.*

Christmas shopping—Secret Santa.

I winced. Damn it. That would be exchanged this week, Christmas Eve, the day after the office party. I had to think of a present for Hamish, and soon.

'Are you okay?'

Hamish. 'Hi.' I placed one hand over my eyes to shield them against the sun and looked up at him.

He'd got the memo about how to dress for coffee with a colleague. Dark blue jeans were moulded to his body, hinting at the shapely thighs that lay underneath. A white T-shirt stretched across his chest, those broad shoulders, and he had a slim black folder tucked under his arm. He looked fresh. Like summer. Like the perfect mix of casual and business, wrapped in one delicious package.

'Are you okay?' he asked again, concern in his blue eyes.

Damn it. 'Fine,' I said, and did that sound mean? Aggressive? I softened my tone. 'I mean, I'm okay. Doing ... whatever.' I waved my hand as if it could say the words I couldn't. Words like *You look good enough to eat* and *What was that kiss, anyway?* and *Is this a meeting or a date?*

Ever since the kiss, Hamish had tried to bring it up with me in the office, but I'd shut him down each time. He'd kissed me, then walked away. Not only that, but getting involved with a colleague was a bad idea.

Case in point—Chad.

Hamish gestured toward the cafe. 'Let's get you some caffeine and talk, then you can be on your way.'

Yes. A meeting.

It was most definitely a meeting.

I followed him into the sea of crowded tables. Miraculously, a couple stood just as he reached the middle of the mass, as if everything really was that easy for him. Tables opened up. Clients handed over their business.

Colleagues threw themselves at him in elevators.

'Breakfast, or just some coffee?' the waitress asked, wiping down the table as we sat.

'Just coffee—'

'Breakfast,' Hamish said at the same time.

Heat flushed my cheeks.

'How about I grab you some menus and then you can decide,' the waitress said, rushing off and returning a few seconds later with two cardboard printouts. She took our drink orders then disappeared again as she was called over to another table, more hungry and thirsty patrons desperate for her attention.

'You can have breakfast.' I shoved the menu toward Hamish. 'I just thought—'

'It's fine.' He gave an easy smile. 'You want to get down to business. I get it.'

I don't know what I want. 'Sure,' I replied, nodding to the folder still tucked under his arm. 'So what'd the contract say?'

Hamish placed the folder on the table. 'As far as I can see, the client can't get out of it unless Murphy's make a mistake.'

My smile fell. 'That's bad news.'

A twinkle lit his eyes. 'But I reached out to a contact I still have there—and it turns out, they have.'

Oh my God. They'd made a mistake?

Could I be about to land the biggest client of my career?

'That's amazing!' I blurted. 'Seriously, Hamish. That's just—wow. And you're sure?'

He nodded, his grin reflecting my own. 'Absolutely. I've got the details for you here, but if you pass this back on to Marie, she should be able to action a contract cancellation effective immediately, enabling you to sign this client before the Christmas deadline.'

I shook my head, amazed. He did this—he did this for me. So I could get a key client. And at a time when so much was on the line. 'Thank you,' I said. 'I just—wow. I can't believe you did all this when you didn't even have to. When you won't even get anything out of it. It's for me. I just—thank you!'

Something flickered in his eyes. His smile faltered. He opened his mouth as if to speak. Was everything okay?

'Any breakfast?' the waitress asked. She placed our drinks down on the table and the delicious chocolatey scent of coffee hit me.

'Yes,' I said, suddenly hungry for more time with this man. Why shouldn't we have breakfast? He'd just done me a favour that would potentially change the course of my career, and would certainly change my imminent financial problems—the least I could do was share a piece of toast with him.

I quickly scanned the menu, ordering the Bircher muesli, and Hamish asked for a BLT. The waitress disappeared, and we were alone again, in the midst of hundreds of others.

I sipped at my coffee, studying the man opposite me.

When he first came to In The Lead, I'd decided we couldn't be friends. He was sexy, ambitious, and flirty—too flirty. Every word that came out of his mouth had sounded good, but I'd seen him for what he was: looking to come out on top. Putting himself first.

He was exactly like Chad.

And I wasn't going to make that mistake again.

I'd ignored his attempts to charm me, brushing him off as just another blow-in trying to climb the corporate ladder.

But what if he was more?

What if he wasn't just about getting himself ahead—but about wanting me to get ahead too? He'd shared Actron with me, after all. What if he was nothing like my ex, who'd always put himself first?

'What are you thinking?' Hamish asked, that easy smile back in place.

'Just ... about you.' I shook my head. 'You're not who I thought you were.'

'I take it that's a good thing,' he said, leaning forward.

'It's a very good thing.' I took another sip of my coffee. A woman carrying too many bags of shopping bustled past, knocking into my shoulder.

'Sorry, love.' She winced, pulling the unruly bag back in line.

'It's fine.' I waved her away. 'It's Christmas.'

She nodded her thanks and kept moving.

'You really like Christmas, huh?' Hamish asked when we were alone again.

'I do. I love it so much—have ever since I was a kid.' I beamed. 'It just reminds me of spending time with my family, and eating too much, and long, lazy afternoons spent lying on the beach...'

'Eating prawns and then somehow finding room to fit in a roast dinner?' Hamish smiled.

'Yes! And pavlova and pudding for dessert.' The hot and cold, the past and the present—the perfect mishmash of cultures in a meal that somehow fit the day and our country so well.

He gave me a cheeky look, a dimple popping in his cheek. 'Do you have any weird family Christmas traditions?'

'Ha! What do you mean?'

'Some people have them. Zeb, at work?'

'Yeah?' I asked.

'He goes skinny-dipping with his cousins every Christmas Eve.'

My jaw dropped. 'You're kidding. But he seems so straitlaced.'

'I know.' Hamish nodded. 'It's always the quiet ones you have to watch.' He gave me a look that was laced with something more, something that made my skin buzz. Something that said he was watching me.

I leaned closer. 'Well, I don't know if it's really weird, but when I was a kid, Mum used to buy me a new decoration for my tree every year.'

'Like a bauble?'

'Yes, but an extravagant one. She'd find something unique, something special, and she'd add it to my gift. Her way of trying to ensure each Christmas was more beautiful than the last.' I smiled, thinking of the gold Christmas angel she'd given me last year, the quilted turtle dove the year before that.

'That's a really nice idea,' Hamish said, thoughtful.

'Does your family do anything like that?'

'Not really.' He paused, then his face split into a wide grin. 'Well, actually, there is this one thing.'

'What's that?'

'My brother and I used to play Christmas pranks on each other. We'd find the worst-taste gifts we could and put them under the tree.'

I laughed. 'That sounds horrible!'

He shrugged. 'It was never anything mean. Think ugly Christmas sweaters—lumps of coal—that kind of stuff.'

'Sounds ... kind of fun.' I made a face. 'I think I prefer my mum's tradition, though.'

'I think I do too.' He laughed, and the full, rich sound made me want to laugh along with him. 'Do your parents live around here?'

'No.' I shook my head. 'Every Christmas Eve, I fly up to Cairns and spend the holiday there.'

'That would be hot,' Hamish said, then quickly held up his hands and added, 'The weather, I mean. In Queensland. I'm not trying to be sleazy.'

I laughed. 'It is.' And what if I wanted him to flirt a little now? What if things had changed?

We'd kissed. He'd run away.

But maybe that wasn't because he realised he'd made a mistake. Maybe he was worried I thought he'd pushed things too far.

I took a deep breath. 'Maybe I was too harsh on you that day back in the office, when I said you were a sleaze. You're not a sleaze. You're—you're not that bad.'

'Not that bad?' Hamish widened his eyes. 'Don't go too far with the compliment. I might get the wrong idea.'

'Maybe you're more than not that bad.' I looked down at the caramel-coloured drink in front of me, biting my lip before meeting the heat of his eyes again. 'Maybe you're actually really ... nice.'

'I knew it.' He leaned back in his chair, a wide grin on his face. 'I was sure I could win you over with my charm and good looks.'

I rolled my eyes, laughing. 'Well, you've done some really nice things for me these last few weeks—first Actron, now Health Direct. I appreciate it, Hamish. A lot.'

'I haven't done much at all.' His gaze darkened. 'And the truth is, you're good at what you do. With or without me, you'd have found a way to land those clients. You're a damn talented woman, Claire.'

Heat buzzed through my veins. Something about the way he said those words...

I wanted him. I wanted to feel that scorching-hot kiss on my mouth again. I wanted to pull at the edge of that T-shirt and run my hands over the firm skin underneath, explore the lines of his body with my hands.

'One Bircher, and one BLT.' The waitress slid the plates on the table, unceremoniously interrupting my fantasy. 'Enjoy.'

Hamish.

I was enjoying him—enjoying everything about this unexpected date.

And when we finished our meal, the conversation every bit as delicious as the food, I knew without a doubt.

I had feelings for Hamish Christianson.

Work on Monday couldn't come soon enough.

Chapter 10

Hamish

Claire.

Her smile, so wide, open and free.

Her laugh, infectious and completely unstoppable.

Her body, so tempting, all luscious curves and invitation to touch.

I glanced up over the top of my computer screen at her. Once, I'd have done that and she'd have shot me a look, one that said she hoped I rotted in hell.

She met my eyes.

This look didn't say *leave me alone.*

This look said *desire.*

I opened my email screen to a new message.

To: Claire.Roberts@inthelead.com
From: Hamish.Christianson@inthelead.com
Subject: Christmas party
Dear Claire,
Will you be attending the Christmas party tonight?
From Hamish

To: Hamish.Christianson@inthelead .com
From: Claire.Roberts@inthelead.co m
Subject: I'll be there with bells on
Dear Hamish,
Of course, I will. I love Christmas, and it is a party celebrating the event's very nature, right?
From Claire

To: Claire.Roberts@inthelead.com
From: Hamish.Christianson@inthele ad.com
Subject: What else will you be wearing?
Dear Claire,
You do love Christmas. I have to admit, you're bringing me around to the event, too. It's been a while since I found myself looking at ugly Christmas sweaters, but you brought that joy back to me.
Thank you.
From Hamish

To: Hamish.Christianson@inthelead .com

From: Claire.Roberts@inthelead.com
Subject: Why do you want to know?
Hamish,
I must apologise to your poor brother in advance then. When he sees the torture you no doubt now plan to unleash on him, he's going to wish I never reminded you of your twisted tradition.
Claire

To: Claire.Roberts@inthelead.com
From: Hamish.Christianson@inthelead.com
Subject: Because it's my dream to unwrap you. And I want to know what I should imagine tearing from your body, Claire. You won't have to apologise to my brother.

The cursor blinked, waiting for me to finish the email. Finish what I'd started.

Was I ready to tell her? Could I go there?

I glanced up at those green eyes again. They were fixed on the screen, the picture of concentration.

I ran one hand through my hair, sighed. It had been so long since I'd done this—flirted, hoped, wished for something more—and I'd forgotten that it would come to this point. The point where it became more than just thoughts of hot kisses. The point where it became more than laughter over brunch. The point where it became *more.*

I glanced at the date. *A little more than a year...*

Nausea churned my guts. Pain, raw and real, stabbed me in the chest, a physical ache just as deep and twisted as the emotional one. *Damn it.*

'Claire? Hamish?'

I looked up. Frank waltzed over, dwarfing a piece of paper in his giant hands.

I minimised the email screen. There was no point dwelling on the past. I had to move forward—take action. Just like I'd done ever since the accident, and just like I'd keep on doing. I focused on my boss, my eyes trained on his dark eyes. On now.

'I just got the signed Actron contract. Well done, you two! Commission has been split, and it's a neck and neck race for who'll come out on top this month.' He slapped the piece of paper against the corner of my desk. 'Maybe you'll let Claire come first, hey?'

I have every intention of it. When I explore her body with my mouth, trace those curves with my fingers, she will be the first to come, there's no doubt about that.

I give him what I hope is my best 'good ol' boy' smile. 'She's a very deserving lady.'

'That she is, that she is.' Frank clapped me on the back. I glanced at Claire. Her cheeks were the colour of candy canes, all red and white together. I stifled a smile. So she hadn't missed my innuendo. 'How are things coming along with Health Direct?'

'Good,' Claire said, her voice pure professionalism. 'We have sent them the contract and outlined the schedule Murphy's failed to meet. It's just a matter of time before they sign on with us.'

It was little more than a technicality—just a glitch in their social media programming, I had no doubt. But they'd promised daily posts on social media, and on the day of the layoffs, one had been missing. It was enough to get them out of the contract, and enough to get us in with the client who could truly make or break us.

I just had to hope Claire would share that with me, as I had her.

'I see. Well, keep up the good work, you two, and I hope you manage to relax a little and enjoy the Christmas party tonight. It's great to see what you can achieve as a team.'

He walked away, humming under his breath.

His words lingered. *As a team.*

Memories flashed in my mind. The passion in her voice as she gave her presentation.

The laughter on her lips as she teased me about my Christmas tradition.

The fire in her eyes as she moved close to kiss me.

This was more than just flirting. More than just an accidental kiss after months of heated tension.

It was time to see what we could achieve as a team.

To: Claire.Roberts@inthelead.com
From: Hamish.Christianson@inthelead.com
Subject: Confession
You won't have to apologise to my brother.
He's dead.

Chapter 11

Claire

You won't have to apologise to my brother.
He's dead.
I read the words over and over. A chill ran through my body, just as it had back in the office, and I rubbed one hand against my upper arm to ward off the department store's air-conditioning.

Hamish's brother had died.

I couldn't begin to imagine how hard that must have been.

When he told me, our flirty email exchange had stopped. I didn't know what to say—did he want me to ask for more information? Did he want to talk about it?

In the end, I did the only thing that felt right. I walked to his desk and placed my hand over his, hoping he could read all the words I wanted to speak in my eyes. All the *I'm sorry.* All the *no one should have to go through this.*

I bit down on my lower lip, studying the gift items in the department store. Secret Santa exchange was tomorrow, and I finally knew what to get him. I just hoped he knew that I meant it as something ... nice. Something that would make him smile.

As I walked the gift up to the counter, my phone buzzed in my purse and I pulled it out. Vi.

'Hey hon,' I greeted her, twisting to squeeze past a giant bauble display.

'Hi. Where are you?'

'Getting my Secret Santa present all wrapped up,' I said, standing at the end of a five-deep line. Ah, the Christmas rush. Even waiting didn't make me mad. 'You?'

'I'm just heading for a blow-wave. Wanted to see if you were interested in getting your hair fixed before the party tonight.'

The party.

The work Christmas party—something I put in a cursory appearance at, then left well before the clock struck twelve. It was possibly the only part of this time of year I didn't love.

But not tonight.

Anticipation hummed in my veins. For the first time in a long time, I was actually looking forward to the Christmas party.

Tonight, Hamish would be there.

And I couldn't wait to talk to him again.

'Claire? Your hair?' Vi pressed.

'Shoot, sorry. I'm going to leave it—thanks anyway,' I said, stepping forward as the line moved. 'By the time I get home, I won't have long to get ready.'

And I can't afford it.

I didn't want to say it aloud in case she worried, but my bank account was looking scarily low. Thank God Mum and Dad had paid for my flights back home for Christmas. I needed Chad to come through with that money, and fast.

'No worries,' Vi said, her voice light. 'Besides, I guess what's the point in getting your hair done when Hamish is just going to mess it all up when the party ends?'

Heat flushed over my chest. 'Vi!'

'What?'

'Hamish and I—it's not like—We don't—' How did she even know?

'Claire, it's written all over your face every time you two make eye contact. There's so much sexual tension between the two of you, the rest of us go home and have cold showers.'

Oh, God. Was it that transparent?

'Besides, he's made it pretty clear from day one that he's been interested in you. It hardly comes as a surprise,' she continued, hammering those final nails into the coffin of my embarrassment one at a time.

'So everybody knows.' I tried to keep the waver out of my voice. 'Do you think Frank does?'

'Frank?' Vi snorted. In the background, I heard the beeping of a pedestrian signal at a traffic light. 'No. God no. He's clueless at the best of times.'

'Good.' Relief rushed through me. What if this affected my chance at the promotion? What if everyone found out, and the good reputation I'd worked so hard to gain was ruined?

Chad had left not just me, but the company, when he'd walked out of my life. I'd been the one who had to walk into a room just as the whispers stopped. I'd been the one who'd been overlooked as other staff members were promoted or formed teams to acquire new clients.

It had taken me a long time to establish my credibility after my ex left In The Lead in the lurch, and I wasn't about to let that slide now.

Not even for a man who just opened up and let you in?

I bit my lip. Damn it. No. In the list of priorities, work came first. It had to.

'Okay, I'm almost there. I gotta go. See you tonight, okay?' Vi asked.

I nodded, even though she couldn't see me, and hung up the phone just as I reached the front counter.

The woman behind the desk eyed the item as if it might poison her, but smiled sweetly at me as she folded it in two. 'Would you like it gift-wrapped?'

'Please.'

Christmas. Presents. Giving.

They were three of my favourite things.

And yet somehow, the idea of this perfect imperfect gift didn't fill me with the joy it had only a few moments before.

***

I walked into the crowded bar just off Oxford Street, and followed the signs with In The Lead written on them to a room off at the back. Black leather chairs lined the walls, with some of the guys from accounting lounged out in the group closest to me. Clusters of people stood, drinks in hand, talking around bar tables. Overhead, the lighting was low, dark shadows filling empty spaces in the corners.

I stopped at the entrance, running a hand over the bottom of my dress. No one so much as glanced in my direction, all too busy focused on their own conversations, their drinks, each other. *This is so not my scene.*

'You look good enough to eat.'

The voice was low and hummed against my ear. Vibrations thrilled through my body.

Hamish stepped around in front of me, and he might have worn a shirt and tie to work every day, but tonight, in jeans that hung low on his hips, and a blue shirt that looked like heaven on his golden-brown skin—my mouth watered. I wanted him. Wanted him so much my skin burned.

'You look...' His gaze trailed slowly up my body, starting at my red heels, lingering over my legs, my hips, then up to where the lace of my dress met my chest before resting on my face. *He's devouring me with his eyes.* 'You look incredible.'

'Thank you.' I smiled. 'Should we get a drink?'

'Lead the way.' He gestured to the group in front of us, and I stepped out, taking a glass of champagne from a waiter and heading to one of the deserted leather lounges in the back corner.

Here, away from the main group of people, it felt quieter, more intimate somehow. I crossed my legs under the table and placed my drink down as Hamish slid in beside me.

'So this is what the In The Lead Christmas party looks like, huh?' he asked, scanning the room.

'Pretty much. The guys from accounting spend the night comparing stats from the latest NBA games. The women in marketing fail to add up that only eating lettuce for lunch means they shouldn't drink as many wines as they plan to.' I nodded toward a group of five ladies standing around a bar table. One already had her heels off. Another swayed slowly to the upbeat music that blasted through the speakers. 'And Frank will wait until everyone's had a few, then give some speech about how he's so proud of us and thinks this has been the company's best year yet, and how excited he is about things to come in the times ahead.'

'Wow.' Hamish nodded, taking it all in. 'So Christmas parties here are pretty much like Christmas parties everywhere.'

'I guess so.' I took a sip of champagne. The bubbles danced in my mouth. I sipped again.

'What about kisses?' Hamish asked.

I stiffened. My head whipped to face him instead of the crowd in front of us. 'What about them?'

'Do any of the staff members do things they shouldn't at Christmas parties?' A naughty twinkle lit his eye.

'Things like kiss,' I said slowly. Memories from the parking lot flashed in my mind. *That kiss.*

'Things like kiss.' He nodded. His hand slid to the top of my leg. Heat scorched a path from it all the way up my thigh.

'I guess ... I guess sometimes they do,' I said, then took a forced breath. *Keep it together, Claire. Just because a guy touched you, even if he is insanely good looking, even if he is the first man to touch your bare skin in more than a year ... oh, Lord.*

His hand inched up, his fingers skimming the hem of my dress. 'This material is nice,' he husked.

A shiver ran through my body. 'Hamish.' *Don't stop.* 'We can't—people might see.' 'See what?' he asked innocently. 'The table is blocking their view, and even if it wasn't, all they'd see was a man unable to keep his hands off an incredibly beautiful woman.'

'No.' I chanced a quick look out at the party again. No one seemed to so much as glance in our direction. 'They'd see two people who worked together behaving in a manner that was extremely inappropriate.'

'You think this is inappropriate?' His eyes widened in innocence. His hand shifted under my dress, up my thigh. Fingers brushed over my panties. Lust shot through me like lightning. 'So this would be considered...'

Oh, God. *Hot. Everything. Turning me on.* 'Highly inappropriate,' I said. *Keep cool, Claire.*

'Oh yeah?' he asked, his lips against my ear. His fingers danced over the lace of my panties again. 'Because it seems to me like you want this. You want this very...' He slid aside the edge of my underwear. 'Very...' A whimper escaped my lips. 'Much.'

I took a deep breath, and placed my hand on his upper arm. 'Hamish, no.'

As soon as I said the word, he withdrew, his face all serious. *He respects that.*

'I'm sorry,' he said, his expression sincere. 'If you don't want this, I—'

I placed my hand on his arm. 'I want this.'

That easy smile spread across his face again. 'Thank Christ.' He took a sip of his beer, his head tilted to the side. 'So you're just not into risky sex?'

I haven't had sex in a year! I'm into any sex, I wanted to scream. 'I—I can't do sex here. Or kissing here. What people think of me is important. This job is important,' I said, licking my lips. 'And while I don't mind the idea of—'

'Don't mind?' He raised one eyebrow with a cheeky grin.

'Okay, I really like the idea of us,' I admitted with a laugh. 'But be that as it may, these are my colleagues. It took a long time for me to build respect with them, and I don't want them to see me as just some cheap floozy who'll let a guy take her in the back of the bar.'

'You'd let me take—'

'Focus, Hamish.' I rolled my eyes, his teasing smile lighting his face once more.

'Sorry. I get it. I really do.' He rested his hands on the table—both hands—and signalled for another round of drinks. 'But I don't understand why you think you have something to prove. Everyone here thinks you're amazing.'

'They do now.' I shrugged.

'What's on your mind?' he asked, finishing his beer and handing it to the waiter as he brought him a new one.

'I...' I looked into those deep blue eyes, so focused on me. There was no laughter there now, no teasing, no flirting. Just sincerity. Just kindness. 'My ex used to work for In The Lead. One day, he packed up and left—no notice, no warning, no...' I took a deep breath. 'No money. He took all our savings and fled town.'

'What?' Hamish's jaw hardened.

'It's fine.' I held my hands out to placate him. 'I mean, I'm fine. I'm over him now. But at work, people ... I don't think they blamed me, exactly, but all the loose ends he hadn't tied up, combined with a few deals that looked a little shady...' I shrugged. 'I'm just lucky Frank took my word for it. He believed that I genuinely knew nothing about what had happened.'

'Your ex is a dickhead.' Hamish's knuckles whitened as he lifted the glass to his mouth.

'He made some stupid choices. But that's why this promotion is so important to me. I want to stop being poor little Claire, the woman her ex left high and dry, and start being ... someone to be respected. Claire, who's good at what she does. Claire, someone to beat in the monthly sales meeting. Claire, who's better than all that. Not Claire, the woman stupid enough to fall for a man with a gambling problem.' I glanced nervously across at Hamish. Did he think that was weird?

But all I saw was understanding in those crystal blue eyes. All I saw was kindness in the set of his jaw as he said, 'I do.'

'Attention, everyone!' Vi called from the centre of the room, tapping her champagne glass with one of the girls from marketing's heel. 'Our commander-in-chief would like to say a few words.'

Bodies turned toward her. Hamish stood, offering me his hand, and I took it as he led me out of the booth and closer to the centre of the room. We lingered at the very back of the group, Frank's mistletoe-themed tie just visible in between heads and shoulders of other In The Lead staff members.

'Thank you for coming here tonight. You've all worked very hard this year—don't think it doesn't go appreciated, because it does,' he said, nodding, his eyes landing on each and every employee in the semi-dark space. 'And I can't wait to announce the big promotion tomorrow, Christmas Eve—after our Secret Santa, of course.'

Oh. I let out a breath. Looked like we'd have to wait even longer to find out who'd be getting the promotion.

'But it wouldn't be a Christmas party without a recap of the year, so let's discuss some of the highlights.'

A small collective groan filtered through the group.

'Let's start with January. What a month that was...'

Hamish's fingers brushed my leg. Even through the material, lust danced under my skin. How did he have that effect on me?

As Frank started in on February and the campaign that saw Valentine's Day reel in some boutique romantic clients, Hamish leaned closer and whispered in my ear, 'You don't do sex at office Christmas parties, right?'

'Right,' I whispered back.

'But how do you feel about sex outside of office Christmas parties?'

I looked up at him. 'Like ... when?'

'February twenty-six was a particularly good day for us. That's when I hired Amanda, and Mandy, your strict rule of thumb has really helped eliminate some problems around the office, like smoking too close to the building, and parking in illegal spots. Well done,' Frank prattled on.

Hamish raised his eyebrows and looked down at me. 'Like now.'

I shouldn't.

Relationships with people at work never ended well—my own story was proof of that.

But as I looked up at that incredible face, only one word left my lips.

'Yes.'

Chapter 12

Hamish

'Yes,' she breathed as I pressed her up against the wall in the deserted alley outside the club. My thigh wedged hers apart, our bodies together. I pinned her hands above her head and kissed down her neck, my lips trailing a scorching path against her soft, creamy skin.

'You're so fucking hot,' I groaned, my face moving down to her breasts. Desire owned me—consumed me. I had to have her. *Now.*

I ran my hand over lacy material. Her nipple jutted out, crying for my touch. I consumed it. My mouth covered it through her dress, my tongue flicking, licking, making love to that bud, and she shuddered under my touch, her hands threaded through my hair and pulling me closer still.

'Hamish,' she breathed. Her hips thrust toward me, and I wanted to make her mine. Wanted to have her right here, and right now.

No.

I tried to push the voice away, but it was there, in the back of my mind.

I couldn't.

Claire deserved a lot of things, but cheap sex in the alley outside her work Christmas party was not one of them.

Using superhuman strength, I fixed her dress in place, stepped back. Her eyes met mine, the unspoken question lingering in the air between us.

'Come back to my place.' I shook my head. 'I'm about a fifteen-minute drive away, and—'

She gripped my hand. 'I'm closer.'

She marched to the street, pulling me along, and this was a different side of Claire—one I wasn't used to. I'd only ever seen her display this kind of authoritative passion in the boardroom, and seeing it now, her taking charge—it was a huge turn-on. I couldn't wait to see her taking charge in the bedroom.

She flagged down a cab and we slid into the back seat. She gave the address to the driver and the vehicle wound its way downtown.

We didn't speak—I couldn't. If I opened my mouth, the temptation to use it to kiss her, to take her right then and there in the back of the car would be too strong. Instead, my eyes focused on the skyscrapers flashing past, the other vehicles moving along the city streets.

We might not have whispered dirty promises of desire, but our hands stayed linked together tight, our grip never faltering. Our fingers made promises our bodies would later keep.

When we reached her building, I threw a note at the driver and we walked inside. She waved to her doorman, and he nodded in greeting.

The elevator took too long. It was the slowest damn thing in the entire world, but when it finally arrived and we walked inside, I stepped closer to her, caging her into one corner of the lift.

'Now, I finally have you all to my—'

'Hold the lift, please!' a voice called from the foyer.

I took a deep breath. Goddamn.

Claire smiled sweetly up at me, her eyelashes batting, all innocent temptress. 'Sure,' she called out, reaching around my body and pressing the 'doors open' button. As she stepped back, her hand brushed against my dick. I took a deep breath. Everything about her expression told me she'd goddamn meant to do that.

We rode the elevator to the tenth floor in silence, the little old lady who'd joined us offering polite smiles every now and then. Claire just kept that cheeky grin, her eyes on mine the entire time an unspoken challenge. Tension simmered in the air between us. When we got to her room, I was going to make Claire pay for that little stunt.

Nicely.

In the nicest way possible.

Finally, the lift opened, and Claire walked ahead, stopping at the third door on the left and unlocking her apartment. She pushed the door open, stepping inside. 'Come in. It's not much, but it—'

My lips were on hers before she could speak any more.

The door slammed behind us, and I slammed her up against the wall, our mouths a mash of teeth and tongues and lips all desperate for more. I made love to her mouth as she ran her hands over my chest, my shoulders, as if she were as ravenous for each and every part of me as I were for her.

'I need you,' she whispered, her hands on my belt.

I flipped her around, her body flat against the wall. One hand stopped at the top of the zipper to her dress. 'Do you know how many times I've thought about doing this?'

'No,' she breathed, looking over her shoulder at me. 'How many?'

'I've thought about it since the first moment I saw you in the office,' I said, jerking the zipper down and exposing her body from the delicate lines of her shoulder blades to the curve of her back. 'I've thought about waiting under your desk until you came in and then taking you with my mouth as you tried to work.'

'Yes,' she groaned.

I pulled the dress from her shoulders, down her body until she stood there in her G-string and bra. One hand followed that thin line of lace between her cheeks around to the promised land.

'I'd be turning you on like you'd only ever dreamed about,' I husked against her neck.

She clutched at the wall as if it could keep her upright, her eyes a challenge as she met my gaze over her shoulder. 'Guess it's time to see if dreams really can come true.'

As the night turned into the early hours of the morning, she proved to me that they did time and time again. Our time together wasn't a wild flash fire. This didn't just speak of desire and passion—it spoke of that, and emotion, too. Of *maybe this isn't just a physical attraction. Maybe this is something more.*

I rolled to my side and pressed my lips to hers in a kiss fierce with everything.

Lust.

Care.

Passion.

Love.

And as we lay there, both sweaty, satisfied, and satiated, all I could think was that this was the beginning of something truly special.

Chapter 13

Claire

I woke from the most delicious dream—only it wasn't a dream.

A smile curved my lips as memories of the night before washed over me soft and slow. Hamish, kissing my neck. His arms holding me close. The understanding in his eyes when we spoke.

This was the start of something—something big.

I stretched one arm out, ready to pull that gorgeous body back in—

Cold.

Cold, empty sheets.

My eyes flashed open. What the hell?

White light streamed through my window. *I forgot to close the curtains.*

I pushed back the sheets, slipped my nightgown over my head and padded through the house, carrying so much weight with each step. *Maybe he's in the bathroom. He couldn't sleep, so he went out on the balcony. He's fixing breakfast in the kitchen.*

But no telltale rush of water from the shower, no cool breeze from the open balcony door, and no tantalising scent of coffee reached me.

Hamish was gone.

Up.

Vanished.

'Idiot,' I muttered to myself. How had I been so stupid?

I ambled into the kitchen and flicked the coffee machine on, dejected.

A note.

A note on the fridge.

Claire,
Sorry, something came up.
Last night was really something.
You are amazing.
Hamish

I ripped it from its spot behind the magnet, reading it over and over as if perhaps some hidden meaning would come through. Something came up? Before seven in the morning? What kind of 'something' came up then?

Regret.

I pushed the negative voice away. No. Last night, I decided to take a chance on this man because he was genuine. Because he was more than what Chad had been. Hamish wouldn't have slept with me unless he was sure about it—surely.

But the voice lingered as I sipped my coffee on the small balcony. It lingered as I jostled with commuters on the train into work.

And it lingered when I stowed my handbag under my desk to no gleaming blue eyes at the seat opposite, no charming smile as I turned on my computer.

The day passed in a daze. The Health Direct contract came through and I signed it and handed it to Vi to give to Frank, but I didn't feel that usual thrill I did when I landed a big deal, that rush of pride when I thought of my numbers displayed on the board.

You're better than this. You don't need a man to make you happy.

I knew this, and yet it didn't stop that empty feeling in the pit of my stomach. Didn't stop that ache in my chest whenever I looked at Hamish's vacant chair.

Late in the day, my desk phone rang.

'Hello, Claire speaking,' I said.

'Claire, hi. It's me.'

My heart sunk. That wasn't the 'me' I wanted to be on the other end of the line.

'Chad, are you okay?'

'No, I ... no.' His voice was strangled, as if he'd been crying. 'Claire, I'm sorry, but I can't get you that money. Something's come up, and I—'

'But I need it.' I tightened my grip on the phone. 'It's Christmas Eve, Chad. I have to buy presents for my parents. And I don't have time to try and organise a loan to cover the repayments you can't seem to make.'

'I'm sorry. I'll make it up to you, I swear.' He sniffed. 'It's just been a rough month. That job fell through. Things have been tight.'

I pinched the bridge of my nose. 'Okay.'

'Okay?'

'Okay, I guess. I don't know what else I can do. I can't exactly force you to give me the money, can I?'

'If I had it, you wouldn't need to force me. I'd hand it over gladly.' He rushed the words, but it didn't make me feel any better.

'I'm sure you would. I—'

Hamish.

He walked past me, his shoulders tense against the crisp material of his shirt. He sank into the chair opposite mine, his computer whirring to life, but he didn't meet my gaze. Bloodshot eyes focused on the screen in front of him. *What's happened?*

The dread that had lurked inside my stomach increased.

'Chad, I have to go. Just—'

'I'm sorry again, Claire,' he said in that sad-sounding voice. Who knew what kind of debt he'd got himself into this time?

'Just keep in touch about the repayments, okay?' I finished, then ended the call. Ugh. What a nightmare. How was I going to manage this?

By getting the promotion.

It came with a bonus, and I needed that bonus more with each passing moment.

I pushed back in my chair and walked over to Hamish's side. 'Hey.'

'Hey.' He looked at me, but his eyes were cold—devoid of life.

'Are you okay?'

He shrugged.

You're not.

You're clearly not.

'I don't really want to talk about it.' He licked his lips, turned his head back to the screen. 'Sorry, Claire.'

'That's ... fine.' I pasted on a smile, so false. He didn't want to talk about what? Whatever had caused him to disappear this morning? Or us?

Was there even an us to discuss?

'Secret Santa time! Get into the boardroom, please,' Vi called as she walked past our desks, looking remarkably fresh.

I walked away from Hamish's desk, trying to inject some spring into my step.

When I took a seat in the boardroom, Hamish moved into the one next to me. He didn't make eye contact, didn't so much as glance in my direction. *Does he even know I'm here?*

'Afternoon, afternoon,' Frank said, squeezing past the chairs to the front of the room. A jaunty red Santa hat was balanced on top of his head. 'Thanks, all, for coming to the party last night. I'm sure you'll agree it was a roaring success, am I right?'

Several nods, murmured yeses filtered through the room. One of the women from marketing buried her head in her hands, her skin a tepid green colour. Apparently, the night had been bigger for some than others.

'So I'm sure you're all wondering about the big news—the promotion,' Frank said. I straightened, leaning forward. *Come on.Make it mine.* 'I'll announce that after we do our Secret Santa, but I can officially confirm that the sales leader for the month in December...'

My fingers tightened into fists. *Please, please, please.*

'Is a tie! Hamish and Claire, you both came in first,' Frank said, and a few people clapped.

I glanced at Hamish. It would have been nice to beat him, but sharing the top spot with the man I'd just shared so much with was great, especially since I still got that one thing I wanted more than anything—respect. Applause from my peers for a job well done, instead of being 'that screw-up's lady' again.

Hamish stared straight ahead.

He didn't so much as flinch.

'Of course, the big game changer was Claire bringing in Health Direct. Without that, Hamish might have taken the crown for the fourth month running.' Frank chuckled. 'And now, it's Secret Santa time! When I call your name, come and collect your gift.' Frank gestured to the pile of gaudily wrapped presents in the corner of the room. The low buzz of conversation started.

'Hamish, are you okay?' I tried again, but it was like talking to a wall. He didn't seem to hear—it was as if he were on another planet.

'Oh! A set of wine glasses.' The hungover girl from marketing displayed her gift, and a few people snickered. 'Don't think I'll be using those for a while.'

More laughter, and Frank moved onto the next present.

'Is this about Health Direct?' I whispered to Hamish.

'No,' he said, short.

I took a sharp breath. Okay, then. 'Look, I'm here for you if you want to talk, but there's no reason to be an arseshole about it. I—'

'Hamish.' Frank gestured to the present I'd chosen, calling him up.

'I'm sorry, Claire.' He pushed back his chair and walked over to the pile.

My heart pounded in my throat. Sorry for what?

For snapping? Or for what happened last night? For the fact that he was shutting down, walking away—

Just like Chad did.

I took a deep breath. No. Hamish was nothing like my ex. I had to remember that.

Even if they both worked in ad sales.

Even if they both seemed to shut me out when I needed them the most.

Hamish took his gift back to the chair beside mine, and I held my breath as he unwrapped it. *Please, like it.*

He tore at the paper, then froze.

His face was a stony mask.

He looked at the ugly Christmas sweater with contempt in his eyes, a hatred I'd never seen there before.

'That is one hideous top, my man.' Zeb clapped Hamish on the back, but Hamish didn't move. Why didn't he move?

I'd thought the present would remind him of his brother. I'd thought it would be a nice gift, something to honour the tradition he'd had in the past.

Maybe I'd read the situation wrong.

Maybe I'd read it so, so wrong.

'Hamish, I'm sorry,' I whispered. 'I thought you'd think it was sweet—nice. I—'

'Please,' he said in a low voice, his eyes full of torture when they turned to stare at me. He gave a small, almost imperceptible shake of his head. 'Just stop.'

'And Claire, this one's for you.' Frank held out a small package in a white box, a large red bow on the top.

A sense of unease prickled my skin as I walked to the front to collect my gift, then made my way back to my seat. What was going on with Hamish?

'Open it.' Vi nudged my shoulder, her eyes on the gift.

I pulled at the ribbon, and it fell in long drapes on the white tabletop. I lifted the lid and—

My God.

Lace.

Red lace, bright as a fire engine.

'What's that then?' Frank asked, his fists knuckled on the table as he leaned across to get a better view.

A G-string.

A red lace G-string with mistletoe right in the middle of it.

Tears pricked the backs of my eyes. Anger, shame, hurt—they rushed through me like an avalanche. A few people around the table tittered.

'Who did this?' Frank asked, eyes wide.

Silence hit the boardroom like a sledgehammer. Blank faces met more blank faces.

Except mine.

Heat fired through my cheeks. Memories rushed me. Embarrassment, hurt, *regret.* All the weakness I'd felt when I'd wanted to be strong after Chad left.

'This is not acceptable. I will be taking this further,' Frank said, his eyes dark. 'Now, who do we have next?'

He kept calling out names, trying to move things along, but I felt it—their eyes on me, the laughter, the whispers. Just like I had when Chad left, and I had to front for his mistakes.

I couldn't tear my eyes from the scrap of red material. The *personal gift.* Humiliated—I was absolutely humiliated. No one would ever take me seriously. I would always be the woman who got taken for a ride by her ex.

I shoved out of the chair. Tears blurred my vision as I pushed toward the door.

'Claire?' Vi—her hand brushed my arm, but I shrugged it off.

'Claire!' Hamish called, but I didn't stop, couldn't stop. I grabbed my handbag and my phone from my desk then raced out to the street, desperate for air, for relief, for something to make the pain stop.

Sorry. He'd said sorry ... for what?

And as I ran to my apartment, hurt heavy in my heart, I couldn't help but wonder if perhaps the man I'd thought of as sweet and caring wasn't quite so nice after all.

Chapter 14

Claire

I didn't answer my phone.

When the fifth text came through from Vi telling me I needed to call her back, I switched the stupid thing off. I felt like an idiot—a complete and utter mess.

There was no reason to think that Hamish had given me the lingerie. It could have been anyone who worked at In The Lead—but one night after he'd seen me naked, when he knew just how important my reputation was to me ... it seemed too much of a coincidence.

And even if he hadn't, he clearly wasn't interested in anything more than what that gift represented—a cheap, flimsy affair that you could leave behind in the office. Something you'd never take seriously.

I grabbed the note from the fridge, screwed it into a little ball and tossed it in the trash. *Something. Last night was really something.*

Obviously, it was something he'd like to laugh about with his colleagues.

Something he never planned on doing again.

I stomped across to the fridge, pulled out a bottle of wine, and poured myself a too-tall glass, one drink to take the edge off before I had to call a cab and head to the airport. *Now's not the time for moderation.*

Not when I felt like this.

There was still an hour before I had to leave. I grabbed a block of chocolate from the fridge, kicked off my shoes, and turned the television on to a cheesy Christmas movie. The kind where the man and the woman were meant to be together. The kind where there were no bills to pay, no co-workers laughing at you, no men who slept with you and then left—only happily-ever-afters. Only love.

Love. Something I didn't have.

So much for a merry Christmas.

***

Hamish
The call had come at five in the morning.

'Hello?' I'd whispered, sneaking through Claire's house and into the kitchen so as not to wake her. We'd fallen asleep sometime in the early hours of the morning after more sex, more laughing, and more talking. She was perfect. She was everything.

'Sorry, I...' Renee had sobbed.

My heart stopped. 'What's wrong?'

'It's Harry. He's—his liver infection has played up again, and we're at the hospital, and—'

'I'll be there.' My hands were already grabbing at my jeans, pulling them up and over my legs. 'I'm coming to the hospital now.'

I'd raced to the hospital after scribbling a note for Claire and leaving it under a magnet on the fridge.

'Renee, you okay?' I'd asked, holding her close.

But she wasn't okay.

Not in the slightest.

Tears stained her cheeks. Her shoulders shook as she gazed at the poor little boy in the bed in front of her. He tossed and turned, his eyes closed but his body wide open to the pain that tore through it. *Harry.* I ached for him.

'He's just—they can't take him too, Hamish,' she'd sobbed, clutching at me as if for dear life. 'They can't take him too.'

I didn't ask who they were, or what she meant—I knew. They were death, and the future, and whatever came after that. They were the forces that stole her husband in that brutal car accident, leaving her to raise their son who suffered severe damage to his liver during the crash. They were the enemy, a being greater than she could fight because right now, every second she had was spent holding on to the one shred of good she had left—Harry. A son she loved more than life itself.

A son I loved more than life itself.

'How can I help?' I asked, pulling back and studying her.

She took a deep, fortifying breath. 'Nothing. You already do too much. All the bills ... the rent—'

'It's the least I can do. You know that.' I shook my head.

'But we should have had insurance. I don't know why we thought we were invincible, but we did.' It wasn't the first time she'd said the words to me, and I had no consolation to offer. Life was expensive—but as Renee and I had come to learn, death cost even more. That was why I'd jumped ship from Murphy's when the offer at In The Lead came up. That was why I needed that promotion. Because one wage wasn't enough to support me, Renee, and my cute-as-hell nephew who still needed medical assistance.

One man just wasn't enough.

'Mrs Renee Christianson?'

We both looked as a doctor stepped into the room, a clipboard under his arm.

'Yes?' Renee asked.

'I'm Dr Charlton, and I want to talk to you about your son's care. Are you able to step into my office for a moment?' he asked.

She looked to me, a question in her eyes.

'I'll stay, of course. Go.' I ushered her out of there and sunk into the seat next to the little boy who looked so much like the brother I'd lost.

As I waited for Renee to come back, I pressed my eyes closed for a moment. My mind felt as if it had been to hell and back. How was it possible that just a few short hours ago I'd been making love to Claire?

Reality hit home. We could never work.

I needed that promotion. She needed that promotion.

Only one of us could win.

One of us would get hurt.

And maybe, sure, we'd overcome that. Maybe we were stronger than I'd thought, but I'd seen the look in Claire's eyes when she spoke about her ex taking what she believed was hers. How could I be the man she wanted, the man she needed, and also the one to take from her what she was rightfully owed?

'A liver transplant.'

I blinked, looked up at Renee.

She walked over to my chair, a grim expression on her face. 'They want to do a liver transplant. But Hamish, he's so young...'

'Renee.' I pulled her tight into my arms, holding her there until her shoulders stopped shaking, her sobs subsiding. No one should have to go through what she had. No mother of any child.

If only Josh were here.

The thought had never seemed louder than it did right then.

***

'Hamish.'

I looked up, dazed. Frank had called my name, the Secret Santa present in his hand.

Huh. Like that mattered.

In the grand scheme of things, none of it mattered.

I collected the parcel and took it back to my chair. Slowly, I unwrapped it, moving as if on autopilot.

A sweater. Red and white, with a big reindeer face on the front. It was loud, garish, and screamed *deck the halls.*

My brother would have loved it.

A lump formed in my throat. Damn it. *Claire.*

I swallowed down the pain that had lodged in the pit of my stomach all day.

I wouldn't fall apart—not here. I couldn't.

'That is one hideous top, my man.' Zeb clapped me on the shoulder, and I didn't move—couldn't move. I had to be a rock.

'Hamish, I'm sorry,' Claire whispered. 'I thought you'd think it was sweet—nice. I—'

'Please,' I said, shaking my head. *Please, don't remind me how sweet you are. How you care—you listen. How one of us is going to hurt the other very goddamn soon.* 'Just stop.'

She opened her mouth as if to say more, but Frank called her up front to open her present, and she left without a word.

When she opened the box, her face fell. I glanced inside. Lingerie.

I frowned. Who the hell would have gotten her that?

Around the room, a few people laughed. One let loose a wolf whistle. Frank made some awkward comment, but it only seemed to make the red in Claire's cheeks flame brighter.

Her eyes shone, and she stood, pushing past me and flying from the room.

'Claire!' I called. Shit. I had to go after her.

I stood to leave, but Vi grabbed me by the shirtsleeve.

'What have you done?' she hissed, her eyes full of fury.

'Nothing.' I shook my head.

'Really? Because she's been miserable all damn day, and I can't help but think it's because of you.'

'I didn't do anything, okay?' I shrugged the angry woman off.

'You looked pretty mad at her in here a few seconds ago,' she hissed, and what was she talking about? I wasn't mad, I was—

Furious.

Crazed with anger.

Because how could my nephew need a liver transplant when he was only five years old? How could it be Christmas Eve, and yet my sister-in-law be spending more time waiting in the hospital? How did the season for giving equate with mounting bills and unanswered debt?

And how could the first woman I'd felt something for in years be standing in the way of me getting what I wanted?

I was an idiot. I was behaving like a petulant child—what was wrong with me?

Claire wasn't stopping me from getting that promotion. Whether she got it or not—it didn't matter.

Renee's words from a few weeks ago at lunch came back to me. The things that made a person.

Why was I fixated on something so little as a promotion when it came to Claire?

Why didn't I focus on what counted—on us?

'I've got to go.' I stepped around Vi and raced from the room, headed down the empty hall to our desks. Was she okay? She'd worked so hard to build up her reputation—this must have devastated her.

'Hamish. Wait,' Zeb called, and I slowed my stride as my co-worker jogged down the hall after me. 'She left. Ran out the front doors just a few seconds ago.'

'Oh.' I'd missed her. I'd been too slow.

I turned on my heel, ready to go after her. Ready to be there for her when she needed me.

'You're leaving?' Zeb asked, following my about turn.

'Yeah. She's upset.' And I wanted to make that hurt go away. Whatever idiot had given her that present didn't have half a brain in their heads.

'Huh. But Frank's about to announce the promotion.'

'I don't care.'

'Your call, man.' Zeb's footsteps stopped outside the boardroom. 'Talk about overreacting though. If I'd known giving her that cheap G-string would freak her out so much...'

I stopped.

Gritted my teeth.

'What did you say?' I growled.

'The lingerie. She overreacted—typical chick. It was meant as a joke—her ex used to say the only thing she liked more than Christmas was sex, and I thought—'

I didn't think—my body went on autopilot.

I whirled around, drew my fist, and punched Zeb in the face.

'Fuck!' He staggered back, clutching at his nose. Blood oozed between his fingers.

Oh no. What had I done?

'What the hell was that for?'

'Don't talk about her that way,' I said.

People poured out of the boardroom, a clamour of noise with them. My fist throbbed.

'I think you broke my nose over that bitch,' Zeb groaned.

'What is going on?' *Frank.*

I turned to the man in question, shaking my fist to relieve the pain. I shouldn't have done that. But disrespecting her like that—I'd let my emotions get the better of me. And this wasn't the time or the place. 'I'm sorry for doing that.'

Frank raised his eyebrows. 'I see. Zeb?'

'He's a psychopath! Turned around and hit me for no goddamn reason.'

Frank sighed, a long exhale through his nostrils. 'We have a zero-tolerance policy for violence in this company, Hamish. Zero.'

I pressed my eyes closed. No. No, no, *no*. How had I gone from nearly having it all to losing it all in a few minutes?

'This is inexcusable.' His cool eyes met my own. 'It's a shame, Hamish. You were an asset to this company, but I can't condone violence. Not ever.'

I tightened my lips into a scowl. 'I understand.'

I made my way to my desk, and packed my personal effects into a box. I shouldn't have been so stupid. I should have thought things through.

But as I pictured Zeb's face, heard the tone in his voice as he laughed at the woman I cared for so much, I couldn't find the regret I should have. He'd disrespected her, and that wasn't something I could stand and let slide.

I walked out of the building, a box of personal belongings held tight to my chest. Four months. I'd never had such a short stint of employment before. Where to next?

'Hamish.' I turned. Frank strode toward me, something red and white in his hands. He held the Christmas sweater out. 'You forgot this.'

'Oh.' I took it, placed it on top of the box. Damn it. Claire. I needed to make things right with her asap. 'Thanks.'

'It's okay. For what it's worth, I'm sorry to see you go.' He pursed his lips. 'I don't know what went on back there, but I have my suspicions. And if it's what I think it is...' He took a deep breath, shook his head. 'Well, I'll have lost two good employees in a short space of time, but I can't look past either offence. It opens a gateway for what's right and what's wrong.'

He thought that? Of course, I did too, but in the world of media, so many boys still played to those *Mad Men* ways.

Frank paused, and something like regret flashed over his face. 'You know, about that promotion. You were—'

I held up my hand. 'Don't say it.'

It didn't matter anymore.

All that mattered was what happened next.

As I flagged down a taxi, the day's events replayed in my mind.

That call from Renee.

Harry needing so much.

Claire, hurting me with her bittersweet gift and me shutting her out when all she wanted was to get in.

Me punching Zeb in the In The Lead hall.

Maybe I wasn't quite so nice after all.

Chapter 15

Claire

I stood at the end of the line at the departure gate. Only ten more minutes until we were supposed to take off—if things ran on time.

In front of me, a little girl jumped up to grab her mother's arm, distracting the woman from her phone. My hands itched to check my own, but I stopped myself. I hadn't turned my phone back on since I'd left the office, and while I missed it, it also felt strangely freeing. There was no reminder that deals still needed to be made, work matters that still needed to be signed off on. There was no Chad to call me and let me down once again.

There was just ... me.

Me and the holidays.

My chest panged. Me, my parents, and no sexy interludes with Hamish Christianson.

The woman in front tucked her phone in her pocket and turned her attention to her little girl. *Family.*

It wasn't just me and the holidays. I was going home to see my parents—people I loved. Sure, it would have been amazing to be in a relationship, to not be spending the season alone, but was my life really that bad?

That G-string.

The whispers.

The laughter.

I swallowed down the hurt. Yes, that had been horrible, but had I made the situation worse than it needed to be? What if I'd tried to laugh it off? Would they have laughed so hard?

Am I the only one who still thinks of myself as the woman Chad took advantage of?

Once, I would have answered yes, unequivocally.

But as I stopped to really think, I found myself wondering. In the last year, I'd worked hard to rebuild my reputation. I'd consistently placed second or first when it came to account management.

There was one person who consistently thought of me as Chad's ex, though.

Me.

That had to change.

That had to change right now.

I glanced at the clock. Nine minutes to go. *Still time.*

I reached into my purse, pulled out my phone, turned it on and dialled. There was something I needed to do—something I should have done a long time ago.

'Hey, Claire.' Chad's voice was crestfallen, as if someone had just murdered his pet rabbit.

'Hi.'

'What's up? I'm kind of not feeling my best right now, so—'

'Chad, I know you're not well. That's why I'm calling.' I kept my voice clinical, businesslike.

'You ... are?'

'Yes.' I sighed. 'Ever since you left me in debt, you've been *not feeling your best.*'

'It's true! I've struggled to catch a break.'

'Be that as it may, I can't support you anymore. I can't keep picking up the pieces of your mess.'

'Claire, it's not like that.' His voice hardened a little. 'And let's not forget, the loan was in your name.'

'But you took all the money!'

The little girl in front of me whipped her head around to look at me, raised her eyebrows. Oops. Too loud.

But I wasn't backing down. 'Chad, this is a courtesy call to let you know that I'm going to take this further. I'm not letting you bully me into paying the debt anymore. I'll hire a lawyer, get someone to look into it, and prove that this is not my problem—it's yours.'

'You won't do it. You're bluffing.'

'I will, and I—'

'Excuse me, sir, no phones at the blackjack table, please.' A foreign voice came down the line.

I dropped my jaw. He was at the casino? 'I thought you didn't have any money.'

'I don't! But you can't expect me to live off nothing.'

'Chad, you need help. I want to see you in rehab, or I want you to come with me to the bank and clear things up. Anything less, and I'm taking you to court.'

'Sir, no phones—'

'You're such a fucking bitch, Claire.' Chad's voice was hard, cruel. 'What happened to the caring woman who loved me?'

'Rehab, or a trip to the bank first thing in the new year,' I issued my ultimatum. 'And as for the woman who loved you? She's still here.' I stepped forward as the line moved closer to the plane. 'Only now I love someone else.'

I clicked the button to end the call. *Me.* I loved myself, and I had too much self-respect to let this arsehole get away with taking advantage of me again and again. I was better than that. I had to be better than that.

I looked down at my phone screen. Four minutes to go.

There was someone else I should call. Someone who deserved the benefit of the doubt.

He ran out on me this morning—he brushed me off at work—but maybe the gift I gave him was too soon. Maybe he felt about that like I had about the lingerie—as if it was shining a spotlight on my insecurities for the world to see. As if it made me less.

I had to do it—I had to call him.

Nervous energy raced through my body as I dialled Hamish's number.

The phone rang.

The noise sounded so very loud in my ear.

'Hi. You have reached the phone of...' The automated recording clicked in.

'Damn it,' I whispered. I'd have to call back when we landed. The line shuffled forward.

'Claire!'

I froze mid-step.

Was that...?

'Claire!'

I turned around.

Hamish.

He rushed toward me. He ducked past families huddled around suitcases, businesspeople talking on their phones, and slowed at my side, his chest rising and falling at a rapid pace.

'What are you...?' I shook my head. 'Hamish, I tried calling you. I—'

'No. Whatever you're about to say, just let me speak first.' He shook his head, a deep earnestness in his eyes. 'Claire, I haven't gone about things the right way when it comes to us. Last night, I got carried away—but that's not how a woman like you deserves to be treated. You deserve the respect you told me you wanted from the people you work with, and I didn't honour that.'

'It takes two, Hamish.' She gave a small smile. 'I don't seem to remember suggesting we stop.'

'Maybe so, but I rushed in. I was so sure of how I felt that I didn't stop to think about the future. And when I did—I didn't handle it well.' He shoved his hands in the pockets of his suit pants. Had he come here straight from work? 'I left early this morning because I got a text from my sister-in-law saying my nephew was sick. I've been supporting her and my brother's son ever since he passed away last year.'

'What?' My God. His brother had left behind a wife and child? 'I'm so sorry to hear that.'

'And that's just it.' He met my gaze, scooped his hand along my jaw to cup my cheek. 'You don't need to be sorry. But you needed to know that—that I'm supporting another family. That my life will always be twisted with theirs, no matter what.'

'That's okay.' That was more than okay. It was who he was—a part of him.

'And that I'm not over my brother's death. I try act like I am, but sometimes, days like this—I can't handle it. I don't open up, and I should have told you. I should have told you I wasn't coping.'

'It's okay—'

'I want to be with you, Claire. This is me, putting my cards on the table.' He shrugged, holding out his hands in display. 'I'm not all nice. I'm not all perfect. But if you'll let me, I'll be all yours.'

My breath caught in my throat. This beautiful, broken and giving man—he was offering me the greatest gift I ever could receive. And I was finally in a position to accept. 'Yes,' I whispered. Tears pricked at the backs of my eyes, and I blinked them away. 'Yes.'

He stepped closer. One hand clutched at the small of my back, pulling me closer to him. The other hand tangled in my hair as his lips met mine in a kiss so scorching hot, a kiss that said *I need you, I want you, I love you* all at once. I lost myself in his embrace, letting him share the load with me—but not take it entirely. We were a team—a partnership of the very best kind.

'Mummy, why is dat lady licking dat man?' I heard the small child in front of me ask, and I pulled away, my cheeks hot for what felt like the hundredth time that day.

'Sorry,' I mumbled my apology.

The woman in front raised her eyebrows, but shrugged and turned away. Looked like the Christmas spirit wasn't lost on her.

The line moved again, and the woman in front handed her ticket to the hostess.

'Can I see you when I get back?' I asked Hamish, not wanting to let go—not yet. Not when I finally had him in my arms.

'Actually...' He winced, pulled a piece of paper out of his pocket. An airline ticket. He was—he was coming with me? 'I was hoping I could see you sooner than that.'

'Yes!' I squealed, and threw myself into his arms. 'Yes, a thousand times yes.'

And as our lips met in a kiss that I was sure the little girl in front of me would have disapproved of, I couldn't stop my smile. I had it all. I'd stood up to my ex; I'd fought for what I wanted; and now, I was taking home the reward.

Looked like Christmas had come to me after all.

Epilogue

Hamish

Nice was my specialty.

But sometimes, you needed to be a little naughty too. Sometimes you needed to be selfish.

That was why I'd told Renee the truth about Claire. Of course, once my sister-in-law found out I'd left the bed of the woman I loved to meet her at the hospital, she'd insisted I book the next available flight to join Claire in her hometown at Christmas.

'But you need someone,' I'd said. I couldn't leave Renee alone—not at this time of year.

'I have someone.' She'd shrugged. 'I have my son, who I love more than life itself. I have you, only a phone call away, and always so willing to help when needed.' She took a deep breath. 'But I also still have your brother. He might not be here, but he's still with me. And I think we both know he'd kick your butt for missing this opportunity when it's someone you care about so much.'

I left Renee with the presents I'd bought for her and Harry earlier. He was out of hospital, and the two of them would be spending Christmas in their family home—the one they'd shared with my brother. Harry still had to have a transplant—no Christmas miracle could put an end to that. But he had time, and his pain had subsided. For the time being, he was happy, safe, and surrounded by the woman who loved him the most in the world.

I'd flown to Queensland with the woman I loved after telling her about my newly unemployed status, and just how it had happened. I'd booked a room in a hotel, but after her parents met me over Christmas lunch, they'd insisted I sleep in the spare room, and even though I really would have preferred to bunk down with their daughter, I did as they requested—because I was a nice guy, after all.

Now, as I sat on the balcony of Claire's parents' home one week later, the sunset casting golds and pinks and oranges across the sky, I let out a long sigh. Perfect. There was nowhere else I'd rather be.

My phone buzzed beside me, and I picked it up.

Darcy: *I know you're happy where you are right now, but I thought I'd let you know a senior position's opened up back here at Murphy's. Derek laid off too many staff, and now he needs someone to raise morale. You'd be perfect for it, and I'm sure he'd welcome you back in a heartbeat. Interested?*

I grinned. Looked like things might just work out after all.

'What are you smiling about?' Claire padded barefoot across the wooden balcony before settling in my lap, her hands around my neck.

I showed her the text.

'Hamish! That's perfect!' She kissed me on the lips, once, chaste, then pulled away. 'Wait—is that perfect?'

'Yes.' I grinned. 'Looks like we're both starting the new year with new promotions.'

'Looks like it.' She grinned, resting her forehead against mine. 'I know it's a little early...'

'But you want to sneak into your bedroom before your mum realises we're gone?' I clutched her tighter, laughter bubbling in my throat.

'No!' She slapped playfully at my chest, then paused. 'Well, yes, but that's not what I was going to say.' She pressed her lips together. 'This Christmas has been the best ever, but it's the new year I'm really looking forward to.'

'And why's that?'

'Because...' She pressed her eyes closed for a moment before meeting me with a confident gaze. 'I love you, Hamish Christianson. And I can't wait to spend as much time as possible in the new year with you.'

'I love you, too.'

And as we kissed on the deck of her parents' property, the sun setting on the last day of the year, my thoughts were filled with naughty and nice ways to please this woman.

Because sometimes you just had to be both.

Thanks for reading *Naughty or Nice.* I hope you enjoyed it.

Reviews can help readers find books, and I am grateful for all honest reviews. Thank you for taking the time to let others know what you've read, and what you thought.

If you liked this book, here is my other title, **A Whole New Ball Game.**

Sign up to our newsletter romance.com.au/newsletter/ and find out about new releases, must-read series and **ebook deals** at romance.com.au.

Share your reading experience on:

Facebook
Instagram
romance.com.au

ROMANCE .COM.AU ESCAPE publishing

Bestselling Titles by Escape Publishing...

Discover another great read from Escape Publishing...

More Than a Promise
Lauren K. McKellar

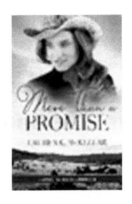

Mindalby, a small town, a community, a home. But when the mill that supports the local cotton farmers and employs many of the town's residents closes unexpectedly, old tensions are exposed and new rifts develop. Everyone is affected and some react better than others, but one thing is certain: living on the edge of the outback means they have to survive together, or let their town die.

Asher is barely keeping her head above water, which is impressive given the drought-stricken land around her. Between her job at the real estate agent, her father's reliance on the bottle, her estranged mother's pushy texts, and her gorgeous daughter, Dakota, she has no time for relationships ... even if Flynn Carmichael is the most beautiful man she's ever seen. But Flynn is only in Mindalby for a short time, and Asher and Dakota have no space in their lives for a man not willing to put down roots.

A Whole New Ball Game
Lauren K. McKellar

She thought she had her future sorted, but life has other plans...

Get the reference, get the job, get out of here: I know what I want. What I've always wanted. What I've been raised to want. The only thing standing between me and my dream overseas nursing job is a reference from my boss—and a very special little girl in the hospice care where I work who I just can't say goodbye to yet.

The *last* thing I need is Sawyer Benson, the AFL legend and an arrogant smile, coming in to visit the kids at the hospice and interfering with my life.

But when Emily tells me that girls can't play football, I know that I have to prove to her that girls can do nything they want. So Sawyer and I trike a bargain. I'll play his girlfriend hen the camera's on, and off-camera e'll train me up for the Women's ussie Rules league try-outs. Together we'll show Emily that girls are brave and strong and can do anything they dream of.

I still know what I want. I can walk away from footy and go back to my original plan. Football and arrogant smiles can't be my future.

Can they?

9 780369 355720